SHADOW
OF THE
MARK

Also by Leigh Fallon

Carrier of the Mark

SHADOW OF THE MARK

LEIGH FALLON

HARPER TEEN

An Imprint of HarperCollinsPublishers

HarperTeen is an imprint of HarperCollins Publishers.

Library of Congress Cataloging-in-Publication Data
Fallon, Leigh.
Shadow of the Mark / Leigh Fallon. — 1st ed.
    p. cm.
Summary: As the power of the Air element continues to grow in
sixteen-year-old Megan, she learns that her relationship with Adam
DeRís—and the combined power of their elements—could ultimately
cause widespread destruction.
ISBN 978-0-06-212800-3 (pbk. bdg.)
[1. Supernatural—Fiction. 2. Love—Fiction. 3. Ireland—Fiction.]
I. Title.
PZ7.F19596Sh 2013   2012025333
[Fic]—dc23   CIP
                                                               AC

Typography by Ray Shappell
13 14 15 16 17   CG/RRDH   10 9 8 7 6 5 4 3 2 1
❖
First Edition

FOR CHLOE, MEGAN, FIONN, AND RÍAN.

I LOVE YOU, MY STINKIES.

SHADOW
OF THE
MARK

One

FIRST DAY BACK

As usual, I woke to Randel's beak tapping at my window. A broad smile stole its way across my lips. I wasn't really supposed to use my air element for everyday stuff, but when nobody was looking, I indulged. With a quick flick of my finger, I manipulated the air in the room, opening the curtains from where I perched on the bed. "I'm up, I'm up," I told him. "Now shoo!" Randel, the DeRíses' rook, shook the rain from his black feathers and disappeared into the dark February morning.

I threw on my school uniform and draped the tie around my neck, leaving it loose. Someday, someone was going to have to explain to me the merits of wearing a tie, especially for a girl. I picked up my bag laden with books and heaved it down the stairs.

"Good morning, Dad," I said, walking into the kitchen.

"Morning, Megan. Who's taking you to school today? You *are* going with someone, right?" Worry lined his forehead.

Three weeks ago, I had been kidnapped and imprisoned on an abandoned boat. Dad believed a psycho had nabbed me completely by chance, a case of being in the wrong place at the wrong time. He could never know about the Knox, their attempt at capturing me, and their centuries-old desire to control the elements. Ever since the incident, Dad had been acting more protective—understandably, but it was still frustrating, especially since I was more than capable of taking care of myself.

"Don't worry, Dad. Caitlin is picking me up."

"Caitlin?" he said, raising a brow.

"It's all right. She has a license now," I assured him, grabbing an apple. "So did you have fun last night? I didn't hear Petra leave." I tried to stop my amused smile as I watched Dad's cheeks get flushed. Petra was the first woman he'd been involved with since my mom died, and she had been featuring more and more at our house in recent weeks. They were good together.

"Oh, she left a little while ago," he mumbled, and then cleared his throat. "She had a delivery coming in early to the restaurant."

BEEP, BEherrr.

The malfunctioning car horn signaled Caitlin's arrival. "I'm off," I said, giving Dad a quick kiss on the cheek before running outside.

Caitlin beamed at me as I opened the passenger door. "Good morning, you."

"Morning. Thanks for picking me up." I climbed into the tiny red car and tried to look confident and encouraging as she pulled out of my driveway.

Caitlin turned up the radio and drummed her fingers on the steering wheel. "Are you ready for your last term of fifth year?" she asked, bopping her head to the beat. She spun the wheel to the right, barely avoiding a parked car.

"Bring it on," I said, checking to make sure my seat belt was secure for the third time.

"Relax." She eyed my death grip on the door handle. "You're going to damage that if you dig your nails in any farther."

I pried my fingers loose, and we made it to the school in one piece. After several failed attempts, Caitlin finally pulled into a parking spot. I caught sight of Adam two cars down, leaning against his rusty Volkswagen and laughing quietly to himself.

His twin sister, Áine, came dancing over to us. "Caitlin! Your car is so cute!"

With the two of them preoccupied, I made a beeline for Adam, my breath catching as I approached. I could feel the dark pull of the magic lurking behind the innocent shade of green in his eyes. It called to me.

"Good morning, beautiful," he said, drawing me into his arms. "You got here safely, I see. How was Caitlin's driving?"

"Creative." I laughed. We started walking into the school building, Áine and Caitlin just ahead of us.

Adam smirked. "It was hard to relinquish you to her. When can I expect to get you back in the mornings?"

"Give it a couple of days. With any luck, Killian will be vying for her affections, and her guilt over his unrequited love will have her rushing off to his place in the mornings."

He smiled. "I'll be waiting with bated breath."

Áine turned around to face us. "Hurry up, you two. Let's get the last of this year over with."

First class was Higher English. We filed into the room and sat in our usual places.

There were two new faces this term. One was speaking in Polish to a group who huddled around his desk. The other, a blond girl, was sitting quietly by the wall. She glanced nervously around the room, and smiled hopefully when she caught my eye. I grinned back. She reminded me of myself at this time five months ago.

When Miss McIntire walked in, she scanned the students with her lips pinched together. "We have a lot to get through before you finish this term. I expect your full attention. If you don't intend to give me just that, leave now and go join the ordinary-level class." She looked around. "No takers? Fine. Now that we have established we are all committed to attaining excellent marks in Higher English, let us continue."

Adam squeezed my hand under the desk and smiled. *So much for easing us gently back into the year.*

The day continued in that vein. Each teacher seemed determined to outdo the other. Finally, lunchtime arrived. On my way out to meet the gang, I saw the new girl looking around shyly. *I remember how that feels.* I smiled at her as I approached. "Hey! You're Chloe, right? I'm Megan."

She flashed me a friendly grin. "Yeah! I think we're in ordinary math together."

"Yeah. The name sounds awful, doesn't it?"

She burst out laughing. "I know. It makes me feel like a complete idiot."

"Seriously. Where are you from? That accent is definitely not Irish."

"The UK. My dad and I moved here two weeks ago."

"You're just like me. I moved here six months ago with my dad, from the US. How are you liking it so far?"

"It's all right, I guess. It takes a bit of getting used to."

"You miss home?"

She shrugged. "We move a lot, so home is where my stuff is."

Chloe was still looking like she felt totally out of place, so I looped my arm through hers. "Come eat lunch with me. I'll introduce you to some of my friends. They made my life much easier when I first started here."

Her eyes widened gratefully. "Really? Thanks, I'd love that."

As we approached our usual lunch spot, the grassy hill outside the school, I watched Darren raise his eyebrows and turn to Killian. "Dibs," he whispered—a little too loudly—as we walked up.

I rolled my eyes at him. "Guys, this is Chloe. She's new."

Darren and Killian converged on Chloe immediately, and she seemed thrilled with the attention. I figured she was okay, and settled down next to Adam. I couldn't help noticing Jennifer eyeing Chloe critically, sizing up the competition. Jennifer considered herself the hottie of the group and, up until winter break, had been on-again, off-again with Darren. But now she was regaling us with tales from her vacation in Marbella, which she had supposedly spent soaking up the sun and catching the eye of an older guy who'd been calling her incessantly since.

"I'm so over secondary-school guys—they're little boys," Jennifer said. "They have to be at least . . . nineteen to attract me."

Adam rolled his eyes and let out a smothered laugh. "You're still seventeen."

"So?" she said, glaring back at him. "You don't have to say it like it's an offense. I'm not the weird one here, Adam! Imagine being eighteen and in fifth year!"

"Hey, I'm eighteen too," Áine pointed out.

"Duh, *twins*," Jennifer scoffed.

Caitlin jumped to the rescue. "It's not their fault they had to move to Ireland in the middle of a school year!" She shot me a concerned look. After the abduction, Adam's guardian, Fionn, had made up a story for Caitlin about how the DeRíses were in a witness protection program. Now Caitlin felt almost protective of the family.

I saw Chloe watching this curiously, and I smiled over at her.

"I guess we can't all be as clever as you, Jen," Adam said, winking at Caitlin.

Jennifer, looking suitably convinced, nodded and continued explaining her mature guy theory.

I felt the familiar tingle of power as warm fingers entwined in mine. I looked down, expecting to see Adam's hand. Only it wasn't. "Áine, what are you doing?"

"Huh?"

"What's with the hand-holding?"

"Oh my gosh!" She flushed bright red. "I . . . I didn't realize . . ." She started laughing. "I think I've just reached an all-new level of weird!"

I laughed and rubbed my still-tingling hand. "I didn't think it was possible, but yes, I think you have."

Two

LOVE AND STUFF

After school, I headed to the DeRíses'. I needed to work on my elemental control and sharpen my skills if we were going to make the alignment— a merging of all our powers into one force—work. It could only succeed if all the Marked Ones were at the same level of strength, and unfortunately, the DeRíses had a seventeen-year head start on me. We didn't have that much time, either. The alignment had to happen on the summer solstice, and so ours had been slated for June. We worked every day after school and on weekends to combat my disadvantage.

Fionn greeted us as we walked into the kitchen. "How was today?"

"Grand," Áine mumbled, petting Randel, who had landed on her shoulder.

I tried to sound a little more enthusiastic. "School was great. Teachers mean business this term."

"Good, good," Fionn said, but he seemed distracted.

"What is it, Fionn?" Adam asked, concern creeping into his usually laid-back voice.

Fionn let out a sigh and sat down on one of the long benches at the kitchen table. "It looks like Lyonis Fleet had enemies other than us."

"Lyonis!" I gasped. Suddenly needing to sit, I plunked down next to Fionn. I hated thinking about the vicious Knox member who'd abducted me. I didn't want to remember his sneering face and stinking sour breath, the beating he'd given me. And the fact that he had nearly killed Adam.

"How do you know?" Áine said, sitting on my other side. Randel jumped from her shoulder and landed in the middle of the table.

"He's dead."

"How can that be?" Adam asked. A deep line etched on his forehead as he handed mugs of tea to Áine and me. "He was in police custody. Was it suicide?"

Fionn shook his head. "He was murdered."

"By another inmate?" I whispered.

"No. It happened while he was being moved to a different facility. It looks like a professional job."

"But who would have wanted him dead besides us?" Adam stared at Fionn in confusion. "Do you think it was the Knox, scared he might blab about the organization?"

The Knox were ruthless and certainly capable of killing one of their own if they felt he'd get in their way. Though these circumstances seemed suspicious, to say the least, I couldn't help feeling relieved. Lyonis couldn't hurt me again. The Knox would be back, but that was a fight for another day.

Fionn shrugged. "I'm not sure we'll ever know. Oh, one more thing. Rían is coming home at the end of the week."

"Great!" squealed Áine.

Rían had spent the last two weeks with the Dublin Order, and I didn't think we would see him again so soon. Despite our rocky start, he and I had become good friends, and I missed his crankiness and snarky remarks.

"The Dublin Order is coming down ahead of him," Fionn continued, "so I'll need you all around tomorrow. That includes you, Megan."

"Why isn't Rían traveling with them?" Adam asked.

"Apparently the Order has some news for us that they wanted to share sooner rather than later, and Rían has work he needs to finish up."

My heart skipped a beat. I knew Hugh had been toiling over the Scribes. Maybe he'd finally made sense of the scrambled writings. Maybe he had found a solution for Adam and me. It felt like too much to hope for, but

I caught Adam's eye and could tell he was thinking the same thing. Was it possible we would figure out a way to truly be together?

We were all in high spirits during the training session that followed. Fionn watched closely as we took turns releasing our elements, then holding them tightly in our control. As soon as Adam finished, I was up.

"Easy now, Megan," Fionn said. "Let it trickle out at first and then build the strength."

He had nothing to worry about. I wasn't fighting to build strength. I was fighting to control it. I felt the power in me, and it was terrifying and exhilarating at the same time. I closed my eyes; with the slightest movement of my hands, my element rushed from me, reveling in its freedom. I felt it as it brushed by Áine and twisted around Adam.

"Good," Fionn said. "Now pull it toward you and hold it steady."

The air around us shuddered and glistened like the surface of a bubble. It slowly pulled together, growing denser, until I felt each molecule submit, waiting for my instruction.

"Yes! That's it. Perfect." Fionn clapped his hands together, then pointed at Áine and Adam. "You both could learn a lot from that performance. I suggest you practice some more." He put his hand on my shoulder as he passed by on the way back to the house. "Really good work, Megan."

Instead of practicing, Áine and Adam turned the next hour into a session of one-upmanship. I sat back and watched the sheer awesomeness of elemental control mix with sibling rivalry. It wasn't until Adam had Randel encased in a perfect sphere of glittering water, and Áine summoned a flock of seagulls that converged on Adam and lifted him from the ground, that they both conceded.

Later, Adam lay on his bed beside me, propped up on one elbow, while his other hand gently brushed up and down my arm. He rolled me over to face him, and for a brief moment, time stood still. Along with my own attraction to Adam, my element jolted in my chest and sent white heat through my limbs, leaving me feeling like I was rolling in a ball of warm, soft cotton. I loved the sensation of our elements' recognition of each other, and it was getting stronger all the time.

Giving in to the urge, we leaned closer until our lips met. Soon we were crushing each other with the intensity of a kiss that fought to satisfy the desire of the elements and our own hearts. The air reacted, whipping my hair up and scattering pages of homework from the bed onto the floor. The condensation from the window surged toward us and spun into a spiraling motion that pushed us together. We reluctantly pulled away from each other, gasping. The tug in my chest stung.

Adam still had his eyes closed. He looked pale. "It's getting harder to stop," he breathed.

"I know." I gently caressed his eyelids. "Look at me."

"Not yet."

"Adam, let me see."

His thick, dark lashes resisted a few seconds longer, before he slowly opened his eyes. His pupils were enlarged to their fullest and surrounded by the most vivid blue imaginable.

"I don't like you seeing them like this," he growled.

I held his face in my hands. "Don't be silly. I love your eyes, whatever the shade."

"It's not the color I'm worried about," he said, rolling away.

I sighed. "Adam, we need to talk about the proph—"

"No! I'm sick of hearing about prophecies that foretell our doom." He walked over to the window, gazing across the farmland that ran for miles off into the horizon. "If the Order gets wind of what's happening to us, it will confirm all their fears. We'll be moved to separate continents to"—he held up his fingers, making quotation marks in the air—"avoid the end of the world."

I padded across the creaking timber floors and curled my arms around him, pressing the side of my face into his tensed back. I knew deep down, this new phenomenon had the potential for trouble, but I didn't want to be kept away from Adam either. The surging power was something we had to learn to control. It was the Order's belief that a union between Marked Ones would spell destruction, but I still clung to the hope of the unnamed pair mentioned in the Druid Scribes. They were Marked like Adam and me, and yet there was little information on them, leading us to believe their lives together may have been uneventful. I hoped again that Hugh's visit would bring good news.

"We'll tell them," Adam whispered. "Just not yet. Okay?"

"Okay." I peered around his shoulder and watched the last of the evening sun creep down his face until he was shaded in darkness.

Three

INTRODUCTIONS

The next day, Adam missed first period. At the morning break, he walked up behind me and gave me a peck on the cheek.

"Where have you been?"

He shrugged. "I had some . . . family stuff."

It wasn't like him to be vague. I glanced around. "Where's Áine?"

"She heard some news and didn't feel up to coming in. She'll tell you about it later." He leaned down to kiss me. As soon as his lips made contact with mine, a wind whipped at our legs, wrapping us tighter together. I wanted to ask him questions, find out what had upset Áine so much that she couldn't come to school, but my brain clouded over as I surrendered into his arms.

He smiled and shook his head. "I shouldn't do that just before class."

"What time is the Dublin Order arriving tonight?"

"Six thirty. You're still okay for dinner?"

"Sure! You know my dad. He's at his happiest when I'm in Fionn's 'safe hands.'"

Adam laughed. There were few people my dad trusted with my safety these days, but Fionn, with his intimidating commando-style presence, was one of them.

"Adam, tell me what's up with Áine. Is she okay?"

His jaw went rigid. "She wants to tell you herself."

"What?"

"You can't let her know I said anything."

I scowled playfully. "Just spit it out! Quickly—before we have to get to class."

"Well . . . since Áine is 'of age,' the Order thought it might be a good time to introduce her to . . . her intended. I guess that's part of what they wanted to talk to us about tonight."

My mouth dropped open. Áine had told me that males were handpicked from a proven lineage and partnered with the female Marked to guarantee the continuation of the Marked line, but I'd always thought of it in the future tense, something that would be dealt with in years to come. "Oh my god. I thought that had all been put on hold because I'd been found."

Adam shook his head. "You're a bit of a wild card in the Order's eyes. The responsibility of continuing the line still falls on poor Áine."

"That's ridiculous! You and Fionn need to stop this."

"What do you think we've been trying to do? Áine won't listen. She's freaking out, but she's dead set on meeting him. I guess she's morbidly curious or something."

"When is he coming?"

Adam grimaced. "Friday."

"What!" I had a million more questions, but the bell rang and everyone rushed into their respective classes. I couldn't believe I had a whole day of school to get through before I could talk to Áine. This was crazy.

That afternoon, I once again headed to the DeRíses', only I didn't stop in the kitchen. I went straight to Áine's room and knocked softly. "Áine, it's Megan. Can I come in?"

She opened the door and took one look at me, and her face dropped. "Adam told you, didn't he?" She shuffled over to her bed and slumped onto the duvet, burying her face in it. A loud squawk came from under the covers, and Randel's head popped out from a fold.

"Sorry, Randel," Áine mumbled.

I sat down beside her and rubbed her back gently. "He didn't mean to. I forced it out of him."

"You probably agree with them. You must think I'm a sucker for punishment," she said, her voice barely audible.

"No, never."

She turned her face toward the big sash windows that looked out over the wilds of what was once a front garden. The late-afternoon sun was streaming in across the room.

"Thanks for . . . ," she whispered, "for saying nothing. It's a nice change from other people's opinions. It's hard with the guys—they just don't understand. Even Randel is finding it difficult to be around me right now."

I smiled at her and stayed quiet, waiting for her to continue.

"It's just this guy, my intended, he's part of my life whether I like it or not. But if I see him, if I judge for myself, it will be me making the choice. Not my family, not the Order—me."

I nodded. "I get that."

"I'm not scared of the Order. I won't be forced to marry him, and I don't feel like I have any obligation— I just need to do this."

"Then do it," I said, tucking away my doubts.

She picked up my hand absentmindedly and allowed her fingers to caress mine. The tingling was uncomfortable.

Wrinkling my nose against the sensation, I tried to pull away. "Áine . . . you're doing it again."

"What?"

"The hand thing."

"Oh! Sorry. People are going to start thinking I'm

batting for the other side." She laughed strangely. "It feels very odd, doesn't it? Right but . . . kinda wrong too?" She turned my hand over in hers, looking intently at our entwined fingers, and then slowly—and a bit reluctantly—let go.

"I think it's just the elements reaching out to each other," I said, breaking the weirdness of the moment. "I'm sure it's nothing to worry about."

She forced a smile. "I hope you're right."

Four

REINSTATED

The three Watchers of the Dublin Order arrived at the DiRíses' house later that evening in good spirits. After we all greeted each other in the front hall, Fionn ushered us to the table for dinner. I could tell he was as eager as we were to figure out what exactly they were doing here.

"So what's the big news?" Fionn asked, opening a bottle of wine.

Will, normally the quietest of the three, cleared his throat. "There have been some changes in the setup of the Order. We have a new task force in place."

Fionn paused and stared at Will. "Why wasn't I informed of this?"

"Well," stuttered M.J. nervously, "we knew you would have personal issues with it."

Will leaned forward. "Actually, they're not so much *new* as reinstated."

"Are you talking about the Marked Knights?" Fionn growled.

Adam sat forward. "The Knights haven't been in existence for over a hundred years. Why bring them back now?"

Hugh, the friendliest of the men, seemed thrilled to jump in. "After your parents died, the Order decided to bring back the Knights to ensure your protection and be ready to step in when we eventually had our fourth." He looked at me, clearly seeing how confused I was. "They are exceptional at what they do."

"And totally ruthless!" Fionn interjected. "That's why they were disbanded in the first place."

M.J. waved his hand. "It's different this time. They're organized, and their skills are second to none. We need them."

Fionn seemed unconvinced. "They have too much say and not enough accountability. That leads to corruption, no matter how careful you are in the recruitment."

I was fascinated. "Who are they?"

Adam turned to me, his eyes bright with energy. "The Marked Knights are a highly trained militia who deal out justice against those who threaten the Marked. Years ago, there was a big falling-out between the Order and the Knights."

"And a lot of people were killed, not to mention Marked Ones," Fionn said angrily. "Hence disbandment."

"Honestly, it's different now, Fionn," M.J. protested.

I gasped. "Wait! Was it the Knights who killed Lyonis?"

M.J. nodded triumphantly.

"Fionn, maybe this is a good thing," Áine said. "We are four, and the alignment is in a few months. Surely the Knights have more reason to exist than they ever did before."

Fionn scowled. "I should have been told."

"The reinstatement was partial and very low-key. Knowledge of their existence was kept to the few who needed to know." M.J.'s face softened. "Fionn, after Emma and Stephen were killed, we had to do something to protect the children."

My fingers laced through Adam's and he held tight. His parents had died at the hands of the Knox eleven years ago, and I knew it was still painful for him to think about.

"You had your own private battle to fight at the time," M.J. continued. "We didn't want to burden you with the news of the Knights. Then as time went by and the Knox activity died down, it seemed less and less important."

Fionn's face tightened. "I thought I could trust you to be open with me, especially where this family is involved."

"You can," said Hugh quickly. "That's why we're here

now. The Knox are a threat again, and the Knights would like to send someone to Kinsale to keep an eye on things."

"I'm not having a Knight anywhere near us. We have the amulet and the four Marked Ones at full power," Fionn snapped. "Who in their right mind would consider taking us on? My word is final. I will not have a Knight in this household."

"Fionn, don't let your family history get in the way of the right decision," Hugh pleaded.

Family history? Adam caught my eye and shrugged.

"So you wanted to see the amulet again," Fionn said, forcefully changing the subject.

"Of course we do!" Will jumped up. "Where is it?"

Fionn left the room for a few minutes. When he got back, he gently placed a box on the table. "As you can imagine, we don't like having it close, as it interferes with their senses, but I've found that keeping it stored in echoed soil dulls its powers."

The soil around the DeRíses' house held echoes of the goddess Danu, the original holder of the elements. The soil's protective properties kept us safe, and now it had another purpose—shielding us from the amulet.

"Really?" Will said, rubbing his hands together. "That's interesting." He opened the box and started poking around in the dirt.

"Will, wait!" Fionn said. "Do you want to show him how it affects you, Áine?"

She nodded, then looked over to the window, where a housefly was busy bashing itself against the glass. Suddenly the fly stopped and flew toward Áine, where it hovered for a moment just in front of her face, and then it flew to Adam and landed on his shoulder. Adam scowled and swatted at it as Áine giggled and flicked her hand so the fly jumped to me. I shuddered as his little legs tickled the end of my nose. Just as the fly got to Fionn, Will pulled the amulet from the soil. The fly instantly lost interest and flew erratically, finally landing on the remnants of Fionn's cheesecake.

"Next time, Áine," Fionn said, reaching back and grabbing a newspaper from the counter behind him, "pick something more hygienic." In one lethal swipe, he brought the paper down on the fly.

"That really is amazing," muttered M.J. as Will brushed the last of the dirt from the amulet. "It's instantaneous."

Áine shook her head. "It makes me so uncomfortable." Of all of our elements, Áine's earth element was most affected by the presence of the amulet. Unlike for Adam and me, the amulet left her both blind and deaf to her extra senses.

Hugh took the amulet from Will and inspected it closely. "It is imperative that none of you ever wear it, do you hear me?"

Adam mock-gasped. "Oh no! I was planning to wear it next weekend with all my other medallions."

Will frowned. "This is not a joke, Adam. The last Marked One to put on the amulet was Anú Knox, and you all know how that turned out."

I swallowed hard as I recalled the story of how the Order had used the amulet to forcibly strip Anú of her element after she went wacko and started killing people. But something wasn't adding up. "Will, I thought when Anú was stripped of her element, the Order member who completed the ritual was wearing the amulet, to protect him from her power. Wasn't that how the story went?"

Hugh answered for Will. "The story is told in a certain way so as not to reveal details of the actual process. The important thing to remember is: NEVER put it on." He smiled reassuringly. "Don't look so worried, Megan. The Order does these things for your protection."

The others didn't bat an eye at the fact that the Order had changed the story. I guessed they were used to it, but I couldn't help feeling a little put out. *What other things have they misconstrued in the name of protection?*

Will's eyes flicked between me and the amulet for a moment; then he pulled the conversation back. "Adam, does it not affect you like it does Áine?"

Adam shrugged. "It did at first. But I've learned how to work around it. I can still use my power when the amulet is out, but the amulet creates a barrier around itself so that my element can't get through to it. Hugh, put it on for a minute." Adam put his hand over a glass of water and

26

drew its contents up until the water was hovering above his hand. Once Hugh placed the amulet around his neck, Adam hurled the liquid ball at him. Hugh ducked, but just as the water reached him, it seemed to smash against an invisible wall and sprayed out around either side of him, all over Will and Áine.

"Adam!" Áine screeched.

"And that's how it works," Adam muttered, and smiled innocently at Áine.

As they continued talking about the effects of the stone, I watched Hugh. He took out a little metal eyepiece, like the ones jewelers use to inspect diamonds, and he worked his way over the amber, back to front, inspecting every detail like he was looking for something.

"And you, Megan," Will said over his half-moon glasses, his voice lower than usual, "is your element still bound by it?"

I shook my head. "I can tap into my element around it, but it's harder to do, and I also can't get beyond the shield."

Will glanced at Hugh. "So why does the amulet affect Áine's element so much more?"

"I think I have the answer to that," Fionn said. "Áine has become dependent on her element. She uses it all the time, without even thinking about it. So the stone interferes with her entire version of normal. She needs to learn how to separate her regular senses from her elemental ones."

"Fascinating," Hugh whispered, his eyes still focused on the amulet. "Fionn, I must take it to the crypt. It would be safer there."

"Absolutely not! I won't let it back into the hands of the Order. You three aside, I wouldn't trust them as far as I could chuck them."

M.J. blew out his cheeks. "The Order won't like this, Fionn."

"I don't care what the Order likes or doesn't like. This is my family we are talking about." It was clear Fionn was putting an end to the conversation. He placed the amulet in the box and left the room with it.

Áine sighed. "Phew! So what's next on the agenda?"

Hugh, who'd been glaring after Fionn, suddenly turned back to the table and his face lit up. "That would be your intended, Áine. I've heard great things, I tell you. Great things."

"Oh," Áine muttered, shrinking back onto the bench. "Do you mind if we talk about that later? I don't think we need to involve everyone in that particular discussion." She glanced at Adam who had his eyes firmly fixed on the table.

"Is there a problem?" Hugh's eyes followed Áine's gaze to Adam.

She shook her head. "Nope, no problem. I'd just prefer to do it later. Anyway, there are more pressing things to talk about, aren't there? Like the alignment. We're still aiming for June, right?"

"Of course. Now that Megan has evoked, there is no reason to delay it." Hugh clapped his hands together.

"I'd prefer to wait," Adam said. "Megan's still coming to terms with her new power. She needs more time."

"I'm not so sure," Fionn said, walking back into the room. "She is much further along than we realized." He raised his eyebrows at me, and I blushed. "However," he continued, "Adam has a point. She needs more time to get mentally prepared for what lies ahead. Let's see how training goes over the next few weeks before we make any final decisions."

Will stood firm. "This is one decision you won't be involved in, Fionn. The Order is already making the arrangements."

"Unmake them," Fionn snapped. "We'll decide when we're absolutely sure."

"No. The Marked are ready, and you know that."

M.J. leaned in to Fionn and lowered his voice. "This is what they were born for. Once it's done, they can begin to live something resembling a normal life. Don't deny them that."

Fionn glared at him. "Stop twisting this," he said quietly. "The alignment is dangerous. We've seen what it can do." I strained to hear the conversation.

"Only because we never had all four at full strength. This will be different."

"Enough," Fionn hissed. "This will not be finalized until we have all the facts and Rían is here to speak for himself." With that, Fionn walked out of the room.

After what felt like an eternity, Adam finally spoke. "Way to go, pushing Fionn's most sensitive buttons. You know, you could have just asked us."

M.J. cleared his throat. "We didn't mean to upset Fionn, but it is imperative that the alignment happen this summer solstice."

They were right. Getting the alignment over and done with would be a huge relief, and I was confident I could handle it.

Adam nodded. "We'll give you our final answer once Rían is here to speak for himself."

"What's Rían doing, anyway?" I asked.

"Oh, just helping me out on a little project," Hugh said. "And no, Megan, I don't have any answers for you yet." It was depressing how quickly my one shred of hope could be destroyed.

Áine took one look at my expression and stood up. "Right, who's for coffee?"

Five sour faces turned toward her.

"Aw, come on, guys, it could be worse. On Friday, you could be meeting the guy you're being forced to marry!"

Five

DEVELOPMENTS

At school the next morning, Chloe was waiting patiently for us at the front gate. She bounded over and gave me a big hug. I laughed. "Hey, Chloe! How are you?"

"Doing well. I baked some cookies that we can all share at lunch."

I noticed Caitlin's eyes narrowing slightly, but she fell into step with Chloe and Áine as they hurried toward the entrance, talking about our English assignment. Adam and I followed more slowly.

"Chloe's too friendly. She's trying too hard." He glared at her back.

"Anyone starting in a new school tries too hard."

He didn't look convinced.

"Adam, stop. She's just trying to fit in."

"Maybe."

"Oh, Adam, come on. What do you think she's doing, spying on us for the Knox? I'm not sensing any danger from her, are you?"

He shrugged, but his eyes remained fixed on Chloe in the distance.

"The last time the Knox got near us, the Sidhe warned us. If Chloe was a threat, he'd have alerted us as soon as she showed up."

"Some spirit guide he turned out to be. He didn't warn us early enough."

"That's because the Knox had the amulet. We have it now, and they can't hide from him or us. Not everyone is out to get us, you know."

"I guess you're right." He sounded unsure.

"Adam, can you just give her a chance? For me?"

He finally looked at me, his eyes softening. "Okay. I'll try to let it go. For you."

He leaned forward and kissed me, putting one hand on the side of my face. I closed my eyes and kissed him back, reveling in the power whirling around us. Then Adam gently pulled away, his hand dropping like a weight onto my shoulder, before it fell. I opened my eyes in surprise just in time to see him slump on the ground in a heap.

"Adam?" I slid to my knees, cradling his head in my

lap. "Adam!" I said a little louder, my voice lost under the pounding of my heart. He was unconscious.

"Áine!" I shouted. She, Chloe, and Caitlin turned and froze at the sight of Adam sprawled on the concrete.

"Adam!" Áine cried, and sprinted toward us. "What happened?"

I looked up at her. "We were talking and he kissed me, and then he . . . collapsed."

Chloe stood over us, looking around nervously, while Caitlin just stared, her mouth wide open.

"I'm calling Fionn," Áine said, whipping out her cell.

I leaned over Adam and hugged him tight, willing him awake. My element pulsated, filling my chest, making it hard for me to breathe. I looked around, expecting a vicious wind or something, but only the gentlest of breezes lifted my hair and then ebbed away. Adam's color returned, and he opened his eyes.

"Adam," I whispered, pulling away. "Adam, can you hear me?"

"That's one powerful kiss you have there," he croaked, sitting up.

My eyes darted from Adam to Áine, and then to Caitlin and Chloe, who turned her back to us as her cell rang. She muttered something and hung up, then faced us again. Her eyes met mine.

"Just my dad," she mumbled. "I forgot my lunch." She looked back over to Adam.

Adam laughed and gave us an apologetic smile. "Sorry

about that, guys. I'm fine. It's probably just low blood sugar." He stood and held his hand down to help me up. I stared in confusion and then realized I was still on the ground. Adam pulled me to my feet. My knees shook, and I grabbed on to Adam for support. What had just happened?

Áine's face was lined with worry. "Adam, we need to look into this."

He shot her a glare, effectively making her drop the subject. She sighed and linked her arms through Chloe's and Caitlin's. "Come on, let's get to class."

Caitlin hesitated. "Is he all right?"

"He's fine. Megan will look after him." She waved her hand dismissively and pulled them away.

"Adam, what the hell just happened? You scared the crap out of me."

Adam ran his hand through his hair. "Let's skip first class and have a chat." He took my arm and guided me back to the car. "Get in—you look like you're going to faint."

"That's rich, coming from you," I said, settling into the car. He shut the door, walked around the other side, and climbed in. "Is something wrong?" I put my hand on his stomach, touching the scar from Lyonis's gunshot.

He paused and took a deep breath. "You know our weird connection and the energy we emit when we're together? Well, it's changing."

"What do you mean?"

"I told you before, it's getting harder to control. Recently, I've noticed that when we kiss, you're drawing my energy."

I couldn't believe what he was saying. "I am not! I wouldn't know how to."

"It's not you, it's your element. Mine seems to be seeking yours out. The pull has been getting stronger, probably as you're getting stronger. I was able to manage it up to now, but clearly I can't do that anymore."

I felt the sting of tears building. "We seem doomed, don't we?"

He shook his head. "I was fine once you gave back the energy."

"I did? When?"

"I don't know. I was hoping you might be able to tell me. I definitely felt it return just as I came around."

I tried to think about what I had done. I remembered hugging him and willing him back to me. Then I recalled the warm ache in my chest and the burst of energy. "Yes! I felt it passing through me."

"Well, there you go." He smiled. "You just have to give back what you take!"

"It's not that simple, Adam. I could have killed you today and not even have known! It's time to tell someone."

Adam pulled me into his arms. "Well, we're going to have to tell Áine. She knows there's something up."

"Why does everything with us have to be so difficult?"

He sighed into my hair. "I don't know."

We sat in each other's arms until the bell for the end of the first class rang. Then we went inside, hand in hand, to face the rest of the day.

At lunch, Chloe stepped over a disappointed-looking Darren and made for Adam. "Are you feeling all right? That was pretty scary this morning."

"I'm fine. Thanks," Adam replied.

Áine noticed Adam looking uncomfortable and came in for the save. "Chloe, didn't you say you forgot your lunch?"

"Oh, um, yeah, I did. I'll walk home and collect it."

Darren jumped to his feet. "Hang on there. I'll go with you."

"Only if you're sure," Chloe said, looking a little put out.

Darren winked theatrically at Killian and Adam. "Oh, I'm sure, all right."

"She's really nice," Áine said when they were out of ear-shot. "She used to do a lot of horseback riding in the UK. She said she would love to come out with us sometime."

"What else did she tell you?" Adam asked.

"Her dad is a freelance writer. He's working on something about the south of Ireland, so he based himself here for a while. They're renting an apartment down on the marina; you know, the new ones overlooking the water. She lived in Sweden before that for a time."

"Interesting," Adam mused. "What about her mother?"

"I didn't get her *entire* history, Adam." Áine turned to the rest of us. "Apparently she loves shopping and has a bit of a weakness for shoes. What do you girls think about some retail therapy this weekend?" Her eyes sparkled with excitement.

"Oh," Jennifer squealed. "All the summer stuff is in. I want to stock up so I'm not stuck with the dregs. What do you think, Meg?"

"Sure, whatever."

"You could at least pretend to sound enthusiastic, Megan," Jennifer said, rolling her eyes and turning to Áine to discuss her preference for peep-toes. I nestled back against Adam and tried to get involved in the conversation. Luckily, we weren't stuck on the topic for too long—Darren and Chloe were back in a record-breaking fifteen minutes.

"That was fast!" Caitlin exclaimed.

Darren, who was trying to catch his breath, just nodded.

Chloe looked as fresh as when she had left. "So what were you talking about?"

"Shopping, maybe Saturday," offered Jennifer.

"Ooohh, that sounds fun. Can I come?"

Adam continued to eye her suspiciously. "So what's with your accent? I lived in the UK for years, and I never heard one quite like that. It sounds like Surrey with a bit of Dutch or something," Adam pressed on, ignoring my digs into his side. "Where exactly does it originate from?"

"I lived in Sweden for a few years." She made full eye contact with him, as if to tell him his questions didn't intimidate her. "We've moved around a lot since then, so I guess my accent has . . . evolved."

Adam nodded, holding her eye contact. I noticed the others shifting uncomfortably and was about to break in and change the subject when thankfully Adam let it drop and turned on his charm. "I love Sweden. It's an amazing country. Where did you live, Stockholm?"

She smiled back at him, probably relieved that she seemed to be off the hot seat. "I wish! No, my dad isn't one for cities—we stick to the smaller towns, mainly west coast."

"How long are you staying here?" I asked.

She shrugged. "We'll see."

Luckily the bell rang, signaling the end of lunch, before Adam could pounce on her again.

Later that evening, Adam and I came clean to Fionn.

He freaked out, of course.

"What on earth were you thinking? How could you not tell me something this important?" He paced across the kitchen, rubbing the back of his head. "After everything we went through to get the Dublin Order to accept your relationship! They'll be quoting passages from the Druid Scribes and announcing the end of the world!"

Adam and I sat quietly. We had no defense. We knew all along that we should have told Fionn.

"Of all the irresponsible, stupid things you've ever done, this has got to be the worst." Fionn spun around and pointed his finger at Adam.

I blushed and kept my eyes firmly on the table.

"And you!" Fionn continued.

I looked up and was relieved he was now pointing at Áine and not me.

"What were you doing when all this was going on?"

Áine pouted. "I'm not their chaperone! If you want to point your finger at someone, point it at Megan."

I glanced over at her with my mouth open.

Fionn turned his steely gaze to me. "I thought you were more responsible than this, Megan. I'm very disappointed in you."

I shrank back into the bench.

"I don't know how we're going to handle this." He walked back to his chair at the head of the table and sat down heavily. "We'll have to be very careful in how we break this to the Dublin Order."

Adam leaned forward. "You're not going to tell them, are you, Fionn? They'll fr—"

Fionn slapped his hand on the table. "You gave up your right to an opinion when you failed to inform us of the problem!"

Adam sighed and threw his arms up in the air.

"What's the point in talking about this if you're not going to listen?"

"It's your turn to start listening! You have put me in a terrible position. I'm the one who has to face the Order and try to spin this so they don't send you off to boarding school in Outer Mongolia!"

Áine smothered a laugh.

"This is not funny, Áine!" Fionn exhaled sharply. "Go, do something. And you two keep your hands off each other. If I so much as see you puckering up, I'll book the Mongolia flights for the Order myself." Without another word, he spun on his heel and marched out of the kitchen.

"Man, there's never a dull moment around here with you two, is there?" Rían chuckled, walking into the room.

"Rían!" Áine squealed, running to her brother. "You came home early!"

"Of course. Someone's got to be around to kick the shit out of this intended guy tomorrow."

Áine playfully shoved him. "Don't be mean; he could be nice."

"We'll see," Rían said, holding his hands out and producing a ball of orange, glowing flame. He threw it up in the air and caught it on the top of his finger, where it spun, resembling a miniature sun.

"Good to have you home, man," Adam said, flicking his hand and producing a blue orb of shimmering water that caught the flames and swallowed them, before evaporating into thin air. "The house is too peaceful without you here."

"Peaceful? It didn't sound too peaceful just now." He glanced over at me. "Megan, I trust you've been keeping up your training—when you're not trying to kill my brother, that is." He winked and pulled me in for an awkward hug.

I tensed. We'd come a long way since his initial loathing of me, but Rían embracing me was way out of character, and this hug felt . . . strange. My element buzzed in my chest.

"Rían," Adam said, pulling him off. "Fancy doing some detective work?"

Rían looked dazed for a second, then burst out laughing. "Shit, did I just hug you, Megan? I must be delirious. Sorry, bro, what did you say?"

Adam shook his head in irritation. "I said I have a job for you."

"What's up?"

"It's this new girl in school, Chloe Nielsen. She's latched on to Megan and all our friends. There's something not right about her."

"Adam, that isn't necessary," I said, but he ignored me.

"Will you look into it for us?" he continued.

"What's her story?" Rían asked, leaning forward.

"She's too eager. She looks older than she claims to be

too. I don't trust her." He handed Rían his phone.

Rían let out a long whistle. "She's quite the looker, isn't she?"

I leaned over and glanced at the photo of Chloe on Adam's phone. She was smiling, chatting to the others. "When did you take that?" I asked, my eyes darting to Adam.

"It's just a precaution, Megan. This is standard when someone new comes into our lives."

"I see what you mean," Rían said. "There's no way this chick is seventeen."

"I've had enough," I said, my anger flaring. "Áine, do you want to pick out an outfit for tomorrow?"

"Yeah, that would be great," she said. "I'm sick of this topic too. Not everyone is a psycho trying to kill us, and the point you're all missing here is none of us have picked up on any negativity or danger from her. Adam, if she was here to harm us, we would know."

Rían looked at the picture of Chloe again and smirked. "Still, I think it's in everyone's interest for me to check her out."

Six

INTENDED

*J*ust as I was unwrapping my lunch the next day, a familiar face came down the school path.

Adam looked up, feigning surprise. "Rían, what brings you to the school?"

Very subtle, Adam.

Rían's eyes darkened as they bore into mine. "Áine forgot her lunch. I thought I'd drop it off." He broke eye contact with me and waved a bag.

"Oh yeah. Thanks, Rían." Áine flushed. She surreptitiously pushed her lunch box back into her bag and covered it with a book.

Chloe looked up at Rían with a broad smile on her face. "So you're Áine and Adam's brother?"

Rían cast a scrutinizing glance over her. "Yep," he finally said. "And you must be Chloe."

"I am," she said, seeming thrilled that he knew who she was. "So you're in college?"

Rían shook his head and sat down beside her. "Not yet, I start in September." Something changed in his eyes, softened somehow.

Adam kicked him in the ankle, but Rían seemed oblivious. He didn't even glance in Adam's direction.

I noticed Killian and Darren exchanging horrified glances. What chances would they have against an older guy, especially one as hot as Rían? I thought it was hilarious and so did Áine, but I could tell that Adam was livid.

Rían spent the rest of the break chatting up Chloe. "If there were girls like you at school when I was here, I might have tried to stay longer."

Chloe looked up at him from under her lashes and smiled indulgently.

"Ugh!" Adam groaned. "Time for you to sod off; we have to go back to class."

Rían reluctantly got up. "Good-bye, Chloe." He offered his hand to help her stand.

"See you around?" she hinted softly.

"Yeah, definitely." He waved at the rest of us, his eyes lingering on mine. The skin prickled on the back of my neck, and my heart skipped a beat. What was wrong with me? This was Adam's brother!

Caitlin rolled her eyes at me as we watched Chloe float toward the school building with a dreamy expression on her face. "What is it about the DeRís boys that makes intelligent women go all doe-eyed?"

"You're talking to the wrong person." I laughed. "But have you ever seen Rían like that before? Too funny."

Caitlin glared after Chloe. "I'm not sure about her."

I turned to face her. "Oh, not you too!"

On the drive home, Adam was still seething.

"Adam, you have to let it go," I said gently. "Rían will look into it for you. This could be part of his plan."

"That was not it. He's gone to the dark side." He stared out the windshield. "And what is with him and all the staring at you?"

I cleared my throat. "What do you mean?"

"You know exactly what I mean. First it was the hugging. And now his eyes follow you around the place. He's acting weird."

"You're just mad that you've lost your ally. If it's any consolation, Caitlin also thinks Chloe is trying too hard."

"Interesting," Adam said. "Caitlin is very perceptive."

"Ugh. Enough!" I turned to face Áine in the backseat. "So, Áine, are you psyched up for tonight?"

"I am," she said. "I'm going to keep it lighthearted and casual. Will you come for dinner?"

"Of course. As long as you're sure you want me there."

"Definitely. You're the only one who understands."

Adam pulled into my driveway and leaned over for a kiss.

"Um, aren't we banned from kissing at the moment?" I reminded him.

His face dropped. "Yeah, I guess we are." He glanced back at Áine.

"Oh, go on. I won't say anything. Just don't blame me when you drop dead." She turned away and looked out the window.

I bit my lip, hesitant.

"Don't mind her. A quick kiss isn't going to kill me." He laughed and pulled me close.

I leaned in and kissed him, but pulled away as I felt him slump. I immediately put my hand to his face and concentrated on pushing the energy back. His body reacted instantly.

"See." He smirked. "I hardly felt that one. Besides, it's worth it."

I shook my head sadly and got out of the car. As I turned to wave, I caught Áine scowling out the window at me. Was she mad that we had kissed? But an instant later, she blinked and shook her head, like she was trying to clear it, and then waved cheerfully at me as they drove away.

Dad wouldn't be home for a while, so I let myself in and headed to the kitchen to make a cup of tea. I was just sitting down at the table when the doorbell rang. I glanced out the window, surprised to see Chloe there. I was pretty sure I'd never mentioned my address to her.

"Hey, Chloe. What are you doing here?"

"Sorry for calling in like this. I was bored and thought we could hang out for a while. I have chocolate!" she said, holding up a bar and smiling.

"Sure. Come on in, I was just making some tea. Do you want a cup?"

"Yes, please, that would be lovely." She sat down at the table and glanced out the window. "What is the story with the crows in this town? I swear that one has been following me all day!" She pointed out the window to where Randel was perched on a low branch in my garden.

I hid my smile as I flicked the switch on the kettle. "I thought the same thing when I first moved here. The birds are just a bit *friendlier* in Kinsale than they are in most places."

"Yeah, well, nothing that a rifle and a few shells wouldn't sort out."

I gasped and looked back at her.

She held her hands up and laughed. "Just kidding."

With the ice broken, we chatted for hours; she wanted to know all about my life in the US, and she told me about Sweden and the UK. She also subtly pumped me for information on Rían, which I guessed was the main purpose of her visit. It looked like someone was developing a major crush. Before I knew it, Dad was clattering in the front door.

"Hi, Meg," he called as he hung up his coat.

"Hey, Dad. Come and meet Chloe. She just moved here."

"Mr. Rosenberg, it's a pleasure to meet you," Chloe said, standing up to shake his hand.

"Hello, Chloe, lovely to meet you too."

"I better be off," she said, grabbing her jacket. "See you tomorrow, Megan."

"She seems like a nice girl," Dad said after Chloe had left.

"She is."

"Is she in your year? She seems more mature."

"Oh, Dad. You just wish you still had a daughter who played with dolls."

"It was only an observation!" He backed away, feigning fear.

"Yeah, yeah, I know. You remember I'm having dinner at the DeRíses' tonight, right?"

"I remember. But let's go out to dinner some night next week, you and me. What do you say? There's something I want to talk to you about."

"Sure thing, Dad. How about Wednesday? I think I can fit you in."

He laughed. "It's a date."

Adam picked me up at seven thirty.

"Well?" I prodded. "What's he like?"

Adam raised his eyebrows. "It kills me to admit this, but he's all right."

"Really? What's his name? Tell me everything!"

"Matthew Stevens." Adam shrugged. "I don't know . . . I guess he's average-ish. He's in second year at Cambridge, London. Seems a bit of a toff."

"Toff?"

"You know . . . the preppy type, well bred."

"Got it. How's Áine?"

"That's the weird thing," he said thoughtfully. "She's totally fine. They're getting on like a house on fire."

"I don't know if she's handling this as well as she's letting on," I said, shaking my head. "She's been acting really strange lately."

"Well, you can hardly blame her."

"I know, but I think there's something more. The way she looks at me sometimes, it's like she's . . . jealous or something. But that doesn't make sense."

"Well, she was in great form when I left," he said, turning into his driveway. "You'll see."

We were greeted by Áine as soon as we walked in. "Megan!" she exclaimed. "Come meet Matthew."

Matthew stood up as we entered the sitting room and awkwardly waved at me. I would have expected a stiffer type, but his light brown eyes had the trademark laughter lines of someone who smiled a lot. He looked nervous, though.

Adam leaned down and picked up what looked like a receipt. He gave it to me as he took my coat. "Here, you dropped this. Want a drink?"

"Sure, I'll have a glass of water, please." I sat down opposite Matthew and Áine and chuckled at Randel, who was standing on the back of the couch and giving Matthew the evil eye. Poor bird. It looked like there was a chance he would have to share Áine. I glanced at the receipt Adam had handed me, then tossed it into the fire. But I caught my breath as it left my fingers. Time seemed to slow as I saw the words scrawled on the small bit of paper.

Anú, Bebinn, Sigrid, Megan.

I scrambled to grasp the burning paper in my power, but by the time I caught it, it was nothing more than a glowing ember. My throat felt tight as I recalled the names. Anú, the girl who'd killed her own mother for a Mark and then had it stripped from her by the Order. Bebinn, the girl mentioned in the Scribes as having had a relationship with another Marked, and who subsequently created some sort of evil being that killed her husband and consumed her. That story had haunted me since my first meeting with the Order in their crypt. I'd never heard of Sigrid. And I had no idea why my name was on that list or where the piece of paper had come from.

Matthew was looking at me now, clearly waiting for a response.

"I'm sorry?" I said, pulling myself back into the conversation.

"I was just asking if you were enjoying living in Ireland," he answered.

"Yes." My brain refused to cooperate and struggled to find anything interesting to say to him. "It's great . . . are you liking Cork so far?"

Matthew cleared his throat, rolling his wineglass stem in his palms. "I haven't seen much, just the drive in from the airport, but it seems nice. Perhaps I'll explore more on my next visit." He started to say something else but yelped as he lost his grip on his glass.

Without thinking, I flicked out my hand and caught it with my power, righting it before any wine spilled and floating it down to the coffee table in front of him.

Matthew looked at me with wide eyes. "Wow. Turns out knowing you guys have power and seeing them in action are two very different things."

Rían procured a ball of fire in his hand as he popped into the room. "Poor Matthew's a tad intimidated by us. I can't for the life of me imagine why." He extinguished the ball of flame in his hand with a loud hissing sound as he sat down beside Matthew, putting his arm along the couch behind him. "Well, isn't this cozy?"

Poor Matthew looked very uncomfortable. "Rían, play nice," I scolded him.

Rían laughed. "I'm not the one he's intimidated by. Isn't that right, Matthew?" Matthew slid his eyes over to look at Rían and then brought his gaze back to me as Rían continued. "You see, he's been hearing all these stories about the innocent schoolgirl turned big, bad demented element. It seems word of your super strength has filtered down through the ranks in the Order."

I laughed. "You don't have anything to worry about, Matthew. I'm completely harmless."

"Unless she kisses you," Rían muttered under his breath. His eyes burned into mine, and a sudden stirring in my chest caught me off guard. I motioned with my hand and sent a large cushion smashing into Rían's face.

"See, Matthew, she's a loose cannon," Rían said, laughing.

Thankfully, Fionn called us for dinner at that moment, so I was able to hide my obvious discomfort. As soon as I walked into the kitchen, I pulled Adam aside. "You know that receipt you gave me earlier? Why did you think it was mine?"

"It fell out of your pocket."

"Are you sure?"

He gave me a look that said he thought I was starting to lose it. "I think so. Why?"

"It wasn't a receipt. It was a list of names—me, Anú, Bebinn, and Sigrid."

"Are you sure?"

"Positive. Adam, how would that have gotten into my pocket?"

"Maybe it wasn't in your pocket at all. I wasn't really paying attention. Don't go getting all freaked out."

"Adam! Anú and Bebinn were raging psychos, and my name is listed with them. I think I'm allowed to freak out."

"Look, we'll ask Fionn about it. I'm sure it's nothing. What was that third name again?"

"Sigrid, I think. I only noticed the names after I threw it into the fire."

"I've never even heard of a Sigrid. Let's see what we can find out before we start jumping to conclusions, okay?"

Not jump to conclusions! Sorry, too late.

I couldn't enjoy dinner; my mind kept going back to the list. Matthew, however, relaxed enough for both of us after three glasses of wine. Once he let his guard down, he was pretty funny. His face became animated as he told a story about one of his "Áine classes," where he learned about her food preferences.

Áine gasped in horror. "That's not true! I hate avocados."

Rían burst out laughing. "Seriously, they teach you that stuff? That's too funny."

"You guys are not at all what I expected," Matthew said. "You're all so different in person. Especially you, Megan."

Rían snorted. "Not quite the raging lunatic she was built up to be? She's a pussycat, really."

Matthew winked at me. "I see that now."

Adam rather pointedly put his hand over mine, where it rested on the table. Matthew clocked the movement and turned and smiled at Áine. Fionn, noticing Adam's hand on mine, started drumming his fingers on the table.

Adam ignored Fionn's hint and changed the subject. "Fionn, have you ever heard of a Sigrid in the Marked history?"

Fionn's fingers froze. "Where did you hear that name?"

"Megan thinks she saw it on a list."

"What list?"

I looked between Adam and Fionn, feeling a little uncertain. "There was a piece of paper. It fell out of my pocket earlier . . . we think. It had four names on it. Bebinn, Anú, Sigrid, and mine."

Fionn's eyes narrowed. "Are you sure?"

"Well, no," I admitted. "I threw the note into the fire—I only caught a glimpse of it."

He shrugged. "The name Sigrid means nothing to me. It's probably just some old rubbish of Hugh's."

"But Adam thought it fell out of my pocket."

"That's very unlikely, don't you think?" Fionn said, forcing a smile. "Now, who's for dessert?"

"I'll get it," Áine said, standing up and shooting me a pointed look.

"Uh, I'll help you with that," I said, and followed her into the kitchen.

She lowered her voice. "What was all that about?"

"I don't know. Fionn seemed annoyed, didn't he?"

"Maybe it was Fionn's note, and he was pissed at you for finding it."

"Maybe. But if it was, wouldn't he know who Sigrid was?"

"Good point. Anyway, don't mind Fionn. He's on edge because of Matthew and me. Speaking of which, what do you think of him?"

"He seems nice. More importantly, what do *you* think?"

"Oh, he's grand. I'm definitely not interested in him romantically, but at least our test-tube babies will be blond and cute!" She giggled. "It's such a relief to meet him and make that decision now instead of worrying about it for the next few years. I don't think he's too interested in me either. In fact, he seems to have the hots for you!"

"Shush. Let's not get Adam going."

"I'll tell Matthew after dinner that I'm fine just being friends."

"What about the Order?"

She shrugged casually. "There's no point in rocking the boat for now, so we'll string them along. Ultimately, nobody will care as long as the line continues, right?"

Seven

NINJA

After everything with Matthew was said and done, Áine was ready for a dose of normality, and Saturday's shopping trip was the perfect antidote to her strange circumstances. Caitlin, Jennifer, Chloe, Áine, and I hit the town with a vengeance. I quickly realized it was going to be a while before my wallet—and my feet—recovered.

"Where to next?" Áine asked excitedly as we walked out of our eighth store.

"How about a refuel and recharge?" Jennifer suggested. "I'm parched."

"Sounds perfect. I'm running on empty myself," Chloe said. "Where's good?"

"Let's go to the Farm Gate, in the English Market," Áine suggested, leading the way.

The English Market was a maze of indoor alleys with merchants touting their wares and tempting potential customers with tasty morsels. The heady smell of raw meat, fish, cheese, and olives, mixing with melting chocolate and freshly baked bread, was a total sensory overload. The Farm Gate café was jammed. The sounds of chattering and cutlery on ceramic filled the air as we found a table and ordered a round of double-shot lattes.

"These should perk us up for another couple of hours," Áine said, pouring a mountain of sugar into her cup.

Chloe blew on her coffee, and a cheeky smile crept across her lips. "So, Áine, what's the story with Rían?"

Áine raised an eyebrow. "Why, are you interested?"

Chloe blushed. "I was just wondering. . . ."

"Chill, Chloe. I'm only joking. He's young, free, and very single."

"I didn't mean it like that."

"Oh yes, you did." Áine laughed. "There's no point in beating around the bush. And he seems to like you too."

Her almond eyes brightened. "Really?"

"Yes, really." Áine looked a little pained. "What is it with my friends picking off my brothers? What's next? Jennifer, fancy shacking up with Fionn?"

"Oh, don't tempt me." Jennifer licked her lips. "That man is sex on legs. Unfortunately, I'm taken."

"You are?" we all said in unison.

"Yeah, Patrick, the college guy I met in Marbella," she said, smiling. "I think he's a keeper. We may even give Adam and Meg a run for their money."

I laughed and threw a sugar packet at her.

"Are you and Adam very serious?" Chloe asked.

"Oh, they're as good as married," Caitlin chimed in. "I could never imagine them apart."

"Caitlin!" I blushed.

"What?" she said innocently. "I'm only telling it like it is. You're attached at the hip."

Chloe was wide-eyed. "Are you sleeping with him?" she blurted out.

My mouth fell open as four pairs of eyes turned to me.

"Well? Are you?" Chloe demanded.

I shook my head from side to side. "Not that it's any of your business, but no. I'm not."

Jennifer and Caitlin looked disappointed with the anticlimactic answer, but Chloe and Áine looked positively relieved. I felt irritation wash over me. What was their problem? Áine's eyes watched me over the rim of her mug for a few moments, and then she smiled and slowly took a sip.

We finished our coffees and hit the shops again for round two of the spending extravaganza. It was dark by the time we got back to the car. The side street where we were parked had looked perfectly harmless this morning but was starting to seem a little creepy.

"Let's hit a restaurant for dinner before we head home," Caitlin suggested.

I was ready to call it a day, but everyone else seemed to think it was a great idea. We packed our shopping bags into the trunk and headed to the main street. I was trailing the others when a hand on my shoulder yanked me back.

I screamed and spun around. Two men stood behind me, one grabbing my bag. I lost my balance and hit the pavement. Before I even thought to use my element, Chloe was there. She shot her leg up and slammed her boot into one guy's face. Then she swung it back down while turning around, flicking her other leg out to pull the second guy's feet out from under him. In the same movement, she landed on him and went to slam her fist into his frightened face, stopping only millimeters from his nose. She dug her knee down harder into his chest until he cried out.

"Who are you?" she roared, her fist ready to smash into his face.

The guy tried to shield himself and started whimpering. "I was only going to swipe her bag." His eyes searched for his friend, who was now lying facedown on the road.

Chloe jabbed her knee into the guy's chest again, demanding his attention. "I'll ask you one more time. Who are you?"

"Pat, I'm just Pat," he cried out.

Chloe's face relaxed. "Well, just Pat, let this be a lesson for you. Stop stealing handbags."

The guy on the road turned over and tried to sit up, holding his bloody nose. "You stupid bitch."

I looked on in horror as Chloe backed off the grounded man. He shuffled to his feet and grabbed the other guy from the pavement. They half ran, half staggered away.

"Should we call the Gardaí?" Caitlin whispered.

"No need," Chloe said, dusting off her jeans. She turned back to us and smiled, all sweetness and light again. She offered me her hand and pulled me up. "Are you okay?"

"I'm fine," I said. "Chloe, what the hell was all that?"

"Oh, self-defense classes," she said, shrugging. "My dad insisted on them. I knew they'd come in handy someday." She started to laugh but stopped when she realized none of us were joining in.

"Come on, guys. You're not going to let those idiots ruin our evening, are you?"

"Eh, Chloe, my appetite seems to have disappeared. Maybe we should just go home," Jennifer said.

Áine remained silent, her startled eyes locked on Chloe.

"Are you okay to drive, Caitlin?" I asked.

She attempted to laugh. "Am I ever?"

I mustered a smile. "Then I think we should all go home. It's been a long day."

Caitlin opened the car doors, and we all climbed in. Nobody spoke until we got into Kinsale. We dropped Chloe off first, then Jennifer, and then we went to the DeRíses'.

Caitlin turned off the engine and looked at Áine and me. "Jesus Christ, guys, what the hell was that? There is no way that girl learned those moves in self-defense class."

"I agree," Áine said. "You're sure you're okay to drive home on your own?"

"I'll be fine. Just remind me never to surprise Chloe in the future."

When we got inside, Adam and Fionn came into the hallway to greet us. "Are you guys all right?" Adam asked, taking in my dirty jeans. "What happened?"

"We had a . . . weird night. It turns out Chloe has a gift for martial arts," I said.

"Someone tried to steal Meg's bag, and Chloe turned on some sort of ninja mode," Áine added.

I nodded. "Honestly, it was amazing. She was lethal. She could have taken him out if she wanted. Then afterward, she just brushed herself off and suggested we continue on to dinner."

Adam wrinkled up his forehead. "Huh. It appears I have a big thank-you to say to Chloe."

Fionn nodded thoughtfully. "I've been fishing around since you mentioned her, Adam, and she checks out. Schools, dates, addresses. All the paperwork suggests she's completely legit. But we can never be too careful. I'll keep looking to see if I can dig anything up." For some reason, that felt like a letdown after all the excitement. I guess I had expected something else to happen. Fionn headed back to his office, and Áine went to order dinner, leaving Adam and me on our own.

"What is it with you and trouble?" he said, lowering his face to mine. My body ached to stay in his arms, but I forced myself to pull away.

"Oh, come on, Meg, just a little kiss," he begged. "I miss you."

"I don't want to hurt you."

"You're not hurting me. Besides, you've figured out how to give my energy back. Please?"

My brain screamed no, but I couldn't resist. I tilted my head up, and he bent down to kiss me. I put my hands on either side of his face and tried to reflect back the energy as I felt it flow through me, but I wasn't fast enough. Adam staggered away, breaking contact. I steadied him and continued pushing the energy back to him until he straightened up.

"You see. We're getting better." He smiled. "I'm still standing."

"Barely," I whispered.

Eight

SHOCKER

At school the next week, the attempted mugging was all but forgotten, though Darren and Killian were so impressed, they followed Chloe around like lovesick puppies. They weren't the only ones with a crush. Rían showed up every day at lunch and spent the whole time flirting with Chloe. By Wednesday, he had secured himself a movie date with her.

I had my own date to go on—dinner with my dad.

I couldn't help wondering whether he was going to tell me Petra was moving in with us. It seemed quick, but why else would he feel like we needed to talk?

Randel kept me company on my walk to the small

Italian bistro where Dad was meeting me. As I approached the restaurant, I noticed Chloe on the other side of the road. She waved at me and crossed over.

"What are you doing in this neck of the woods?" Chloe asked.

"Meeting my dad for dinner. He needs to *talk*."

Her eyebrows pulled together. "What about?"

"I'm not sure. I think his girlfriend might be moving in with us," I said, then kicked myself for bringing it up. I was supposed to be suspicious of Chloe, but she just kept sucking me in.

She crossed her arms, leaning back on the old stone wall behind her. "Wow. Big changes, then."

"Maybe."

"Petra Van Meulder, right?"

"Uh, yeah." Had I mentioned Petra to Chloe before?

Her eyes flickered up and down the road. "You like her?"

I shrugged. "I guess. She seems pretty nice."

"Has she any other family?" she asked intently.

What was with the twenty-questions routine? Chloe must have realized she was starting to irritate me, because she laughed and put her hand on my arm.

"Would you listen to me? I'm so nosy. Anyway, I better go. I've got my hot date tonight. See you tomorrow!" And she walked up the road at a blindingly fast pace.

I shook my head. *Hot date indeed.*

"Hi, Meg."

I swung around. "Dad! Sorry, I was in another world. Come on, I'm starving."

After we were seated, Dad ordered a glass of wine and held it out to me. "To our future," he said, draining it in one gulp. Then he fell silent and started playing with his napkin, twisting it over and over again.

"Come on, Dad, the suspense is killing me. Spill it."

Dad stuck his finger under his collar and tugged at it. "I've been putting this off for a while now, so I'll just come right out and say it." He met my eyes.

"Go for it, Dad."

He took a deep breath. "I'm going to ask Petra to marry me."

I gasped. "You want to get married?"

"I realize that it might come as a bit of a shock to you, Meg—"

"You can say that again."

"I really like her. Megan . . . I love her."

I struggled to form words to express how I felt. "I know, but there's no rush." I looked up at him. "Is there?"

He sighed and looked down at the table. The waiter came over and delivered our first course with a flourish. As soon as he was gone, I leaned forward, waiting for my answer.

He glanced at me sheepishly. "No. Well . . . there was, but not anymore."

"What do you mean?"

"We had a bit of a scare."

"She was pregnant?"

Dad nodded. "She'd only just found out when she miscarried."

"Oh . . ."

"She's fine," he said, brushing it off. "It was very early on, and, well . . . I think both of us are beyond all that. But it made me realize that I want our future to include her."

"But marriage? It's only been six months."

"I love her, Meg. I haven't felt like this about anyone since your mom. And I'm not getting any younger."

"Dad, if I told you I was going to marry Adam, what would you say?"

He shook his head. "That's different. You're so young."

"But you're using *your* age as a reason. Look, Dad, I'd be all for it eventually, but just give it some time. Please?"

He hesitated, then picked up his glass. "When did you become the sensible one in this relationship?"

I sighed in relief. "Well, women are the voice of reason."

His mouth curled into a sad smile. "Your mother used to say that."

"Where do you think I got it from?" I took another sip of my water and crunched on an ice cube.

"So you're okay with me asking her, if I give it more time?" he said, leaning back in his seat.

I nodded.

"How much time?"

"I don't know. Time. Spend more weekends together, go on a vacation, have her move in. That's actually what I thought you were going to talk about tonight."

Dad squirmed. "I didn't know if you'd approve."

I rolled my eyes. "Oh, Dad, please."

"Okay, then. I think having Petra move in would be wonderful. I'm so happy you're able to handle this all, Megan. I don't know what I'd do without such a mature, smart, sensible daughter."

I forced a grin and sighed inwardly with relief—disastrous situation averted . . . for now, anyway.

After dinner, Dad went to Petra's house, and Adam met me outside the restaurant. We walked through the winding Kinsale streets, listening to the sounds of clinking glasses and laughter coming from the pubs and restaurants. The flow of energy between us when holding hands was comfortable, enjoyable even. Most importantly, it was manageable, so we could indulge in the contact.

Adam squeezed my fingers lightly, sending hot tingles up my arm. "So did your dad fess up?"

"He did." I gazed up at the starry sky and sighed. "Seriously, I don't understand you guys."

He stopped and pulled on my arm. "As if girls make perfect sense?"

I smiled. "Don't take it personally."

Adam opened his mouth to retort, but then his eyes narrowed and he pointed to the pier just in front of us. On the old stone wall that snaked its way along the water, there was a couple in an embrace. They were so molded into each other, it was hard to make out where one body started and one ended.

"Wow," I mouthed, turning away.

"Look again," Adam said.

The moon had crept out from behind the clouds and was now bathing the couple in a soft light. The girl was leaning back with her chin in the air and her eyes closed. The guy was supporting her while kissing her neck, moving down toward her chest.

I gasped. It was Chloe and Rían! *I guess they never made it to the movie.* I could feel Adam's disapproval. He turned on his heel and stalked off in the opposite direction.

"Adam, wait!" I sped up to catch him. "They're just kissing."

"I don't trust her."

I sighed in exasperation. "At least have some faith in Rían's judgment."

"You saw them. He's no longer thinking with his brain." Adam started walking again.

"He deserves a chance to be happy," I insisted, tugging on his sleeve. "If you listened to everyone who said I was wrong for you, we'd never have gotten together. What makes this so different?"

Adam stopped and turned back to me, looking defeated. "Why should it be so easy for them? It doesn't seem fair. I want what they have."

"I want that too," I whispered.

"We might never have it," he said sadly.

"I refuse to believe that."

He nodded and lowered his lips to mine for a gentle kiss, stopping before the power became more than a tingle on our lips.

Nine

COMPLICATIONS

ancy a morning cuppa?"

I rubbed my eyes, forcing them to focus on Petra in her uniform of jeans, an Aran sweater, and Barbour Wellington boots. "You look like you could do with one," she said. Petra sat down at the head of the table and pushed a mug toward me. I hesitated, shifting my weight from one foot to the other. Her tall, lean figure looked alien in Dad's usual spot.

"I won't bite, you know. Is everything all right with you?" she asked.

"Fine."

"And how about that boyfriend of yours, Adam?"

What business was it of hers how he was? "What?"

She dropped her head to the side and gave me what she obviously thought was an understanding smile, but it never reached her eyes. I'd always thought they were a pretty shade of gray, but today they reminded me of ten-day-old roadside snow. "You just seem a little stressed."

I shook my head in annoyance. I hoped Petra wasn't going to start getting all stepmom-like, because I was too old to play that game. "I'm fine. We're both fine." I sighed and shuffled over to her. Petra was a no–nonsense woman. There could only be one reason why she was here this morning offering me tea and asking about my boyfriend. The sooner I sat down and heard her out, the faster I'd be able to leave.

"Your dad and I had a chat last night."

Just as I thought. "Oh yeah?"

"He mentioned that he told you about the miscarriage."

A little relieved, I looked up. "I'm so sorry. I didn't know."

"Ara, you know, these things happen." Her hand fluttered to a strand of hair and smoothed it behind her ear. "I had a child once, but . . . well, it was a long time ago."

Enveloped in silence, I counted the ticks of the clock while I searched for the right thing to say.

Luckily, Petra continued. "Your father and I have spoken about moving our relationship forward before, you know."

I cringed. "Caleb mentioned you thought things might be moving too fast."

I squirmed in the chair. "Petra, I really don't feel comfortable talking about this. Where's Dad, anyway?"

"He's upstairs. He wanted to give us a chance to chat."

Thanks a lot, Dad.

"If you don't want to discuss it, it's fine. We won't. I just want you to know that I love your dad. I didn't expect to, but I do, and I'm here to stay."

Whoa. Did Petra just go all territorial on me? Thankfully, Dad walked into the room at that moment, saving me from more awkward conversation. He tussled my hair and planted a kiss on Petra's cheek. "How are my two favorite girls?"

"Marvelous, aren't we, Megan?" Petra said, still not breaking eye contact with me.

"Yeah, great," I mumbled. "I better get going."

"Yes, we don't want you late for school," Petra said. "I'm making dinner here tonight— spaghetti, your dad's favorite. So make sure you're back from the DeRíses' on time."

I tried not to let my irritation show as I walked to the front door.

Dad followed me out. "Thanks for last night, Meg. You were completely right about not rushing things, and Petra loves the idea of us all getting to know each other better. This is going to be great."

"Sure it will, Dad." It seemed I'd just witnessed my advice exploding in my face. *Score one for Petra.*

Chloe was all smiles that morning in school, and I could guess why.

"Well," I asked, nudging her, "how were the movies last night?"

She flushed a little. "Good. We had fun."

Sure you did.

Caitlin came down the hall, beaming from ear to ear. "Chloe, I hear you were getting hot and dirty down at the pier last night."

Chloe's eyes opened wide. "Oh shit, that's just wonderful."

I half laughed. "It's a small town, Chloe."

Her mouth dropped open. "You knew too?"

"Adam and I might have stumbled across you guys last night."

Chloe narrowed her eyes. "Then why ask me about the movie?"

"I was giving you a chance to come clean, which you totally failed at, by the way."

Caitlin looked confused. "What's the problem?"

"I'm guessing it was supposed to be a secret tryst," I said.

Caitlin put her hand to her mouth, trying to smother her laugh. "If you want to get off with someone, don't do it on the pier. And what on earth do you want to hide it for? Rían is a ride."

Chloe fixed her eyes on me. "I know how it must have looked, but not that much happened, honestly."

"Hey, you don't have to explain yourself to me. It's none of my business."

"It's just . . . I don't know how long I'm staying, and if . . . my . . . my dad finds out . . . well, he'll kill me." She shook her head. "Rían and I were going to keep this secret."

I couldn't bring myself to feel too sorry for her. "Well, you should have picked a more discreet location if that's the case."

Caitlin crossed her arms. "I still don't know what all the fuss is about. So you kissed a gorgeous guy in public. I'd take your place in a heartbeat."

The strain on Chloe's face eased a little. "He *is* gorgeous, isn't he?" She sighed and then giggled. "Oh my god, I can't believe I'm doing this."

"Doing what?" I asked.

"Going out with a . . ." She stopped and cleared her throat. "With a DeRís."

"Oh, so you're going out now?" I asked.

"I think we are."

I smiled and laughed but was struck with a twinge of jealousy. I suddenly understood how Adam felt last night. It seemed too easy for them.

That twinge grew into an uncomfortable, curdled mass in the pit of my stomach at the end of the day. Rían, who obviously did not share Chloe's thoughts on secrecy, stood outside the school gates waiting for her. As soon as she passed through, he swooped in and gave her a kiss that left onlookers blushing. I was horrified to find myself brimming with resentment . . . and something else.

Adam curled his arms around my waist and put his chin on my shoulder. He sighed into my ear. "Watching only makes it harder."

I nodded and leaned into him. I knew he was referring to our limited physical relationship and our growing desire for more. What he didn't know was that at that very minute, all my body craved was Rían.

Through March, we kept up our steady elemental practice. We all got stronger and more precise. I now had air manipulation nearly perfected, and moving stuff was child's play. The same went for Adam and Rían, though after each session, they were drained, while I felt invigorated. I could sense my element growing more and more powerful.

Áine was the only exception. Her element wasn't growing at the same rate as the rest of us. If anything, she was getting weaker.

Today's session was grueling. The guys had already finished up and gone in to shower, but Áine wanted to practice some more. "What is wrong with me?" she asked, dropping to the ground in exhaustion. "I feel like my power is seeping away, and what's left is trapped in here." She poked herself in the chest. Her fingers inched closer to mine, stopping when our fingertips touched. Randel fluttered to the grass beside us and jumped onto Áine's knee. "I've been trying to stop my overdependence on my power so I can defend myself in the presence of the amulet, but the more I try to separate myself from the element, the weaker I feel. I can see you guys growing, but I feel left behind." She petted Randel's head absentmindedly with one finger. He hopped onto her shoulder and snuggled into her neck. "If it comes to another showdown with the Knox, I don't want to be the weak link."

"You'll figure it out, Áine," I said.

She arched her long neck over the bird, her dark hair falling onto his black feathers, and sighed. "I hope so. It's only three months to the alignment, and we need to all be at the same level for it to work."

I was itching to move my hand. The feeling of her fingers brushing mine left me with a fizzing sensation, like the blood supply had been cut off.

"Anyway, tomorrow's another day," she said, getting up. "I'll figure it out."

I watched her walk back toward the house, then looked down at my still-tingling hand. Beside my fingers, where Áine's hand had rested, was an imprint of where she had leaned. A perfect handprint of daisies and buttercups. She had more power than she realized.

I leaned over to brush off my jeans. As I did, I noticed another outline, right beside Áine's, where my hand had been. It was another perfect print of daisies and buttercups, identical to hers—only smaller. I gasped and put my hand back over it.

"What's up?" Adam asked, looking at my shocked face as he approached me.

"The flowers!"

"Yeah, looks like Áine's work."

I lifted my hand. "Yes, but what about this one?"

"What exactly am I supposed to be seeing?"

"The flower print." I pointed to where my hand had been, but all that remained was crushed, scraggy grass. "I . . . there was another one."

"I think someone's been working too hard. You've got double vision." He leaned down to kiss me, and within seconds, all thoughts of flowers were gone. I was enveloped by a tidal wave of energy, and this time, I was able to keep Adam conscious. I pulled him onto me, and as our hips connected, I felt him give in. His mouth left mine to explore my neck. He gently pulled open the top few buttons of my blouse, and his lips rested on the hollow of my collarbone before moving downward. I enjoyed every tantalizing sensation. His hands worked their way under my shirt. I followed suit, allowing my own to creep up under his shirt, reveling in the hot smoothness of his back. I ran a finger under the waistband of his jeans and built the courage to reach for the top button when his hand grabbed mine.

"Stop."

"Why?" I said breathlessly, trying to pull my hand from his grip.

"We have to stop." His voice softened as he took my hands in his.

"But I've got the power under control."

"I know, but we're lying on the grass behind my house!"

"So what?" I asked, pulling away and tugging my shirt back over my shoulder. "You said you wanted this. You said you wanted what Chloe and Rían have." Leaves lifted off the ground, along with loose, thin blades of grass, dust, and dirt. They floated around us in an eerie dance.

"Megan, I'm not saying no. I'm saying not here, not now."

All the energy swirling around me came to a complete halt, like I'd stopped time itself. The debris surrounding us froze, suspended in the air. My element pulsated in my chest, demanding that I continue.

"Megan, look at yourself—you're barely in control."

"I'm in control," I whispered.

"If you could look at your eyes, you'd see you're not."

Anger flared inside me. I needed physical contact

with him more than I cared to admit. The tightness in my chest threatened to crush me. I closed my eyes, pushing back the tears that gathered. It scared me how much I wanted him.

"Megan, please don't be upset."

I nodded, still not opening my eyes.

"Look at me."

I couldn't.

"I need you to look at me." He took my head in his hands and rubbed away my tears with his thumbs.

"Please?"

I finally gave in to my tears and leaned into him. As soon as I did, everything that had been caught in frozen stillness fluttered for a second before falling to the ground.

"I'm sorry," Adam mumbled into my hair. "I'm so sorry. Come on, I'll take you home."

I pushed myself up and gasped as I lifted my hand. There, where my palm had been, the grass was dead, earthy brown, and rotted. I quickly stepped on the dead patch and averted my eyes, pulling Adam toward the house before he noticed. Something was wrong with me, and I didn't want him to know. I didn't want any of them to know.

Ten

BAD BEHAVIOR

As the weeks passed, Chloe and Rían got even more intense, but Chloe remained freaked out about her dad finding out, so she and Rían were always slinking off for secret trysts. The sexual tension they oozed when in each other's company was hard for me to stomach.

Because Chloe insisted they try to keep the relationship semi-under wraps, Fionn didn't realize how involved Rían and Chloe had become. All the same, maybe he wouldn't have cared—as far as I knew, he hadn't found anything suspicious in Chloe's background. It also meant that she was never at the DeRíses', which left our daily elemental training blissfully free of tension. I still found myself drawn to Rían when Chloe was around, as much as I tried to pretend it wasn't true. It was comforting in a strange way, though. It meant it had to be some sort of weird jealousy thing.

With April came the Easter break—two whole weeks off. Chloe had gone to visit family in the UK, leaving Rían lolling around the house, feeling sorry for himself. He was sprawled out on the sitting-room floor talking to her on his cell. Adam rolled his eyes in exasperation and stepped over him on the way into the kitchen.

"Couldn't he spare us and make the call in his room?" Adam said loud enough for Rían to hear him.

Áine glanced up from her laptop. "There's a classic example of the pot calling the kettle black. We've had to put up with you and Megan mooning over each other half the time and groping each other the rest of it. Give him a break."

"But Chloe is the subject of an ongoing investigation, which he is failing at miserably. Am I the only sane one around here? What the hell's next? Oh, I know— maybe we should invite her and her family over for the alignment!"

"Hey, that's not a bad idea," Rían said, walking into the kitchen balancing what looked like a white-and-brown baseball on a strange wooden club. "Honestly, bro, you have to let it go. I haven't come across anything dodgy." He started tapping the ball in the air with the club.

"Except maybe her taste in men." Áine laughed.

Adam scowled. "Your relationship puts us all at risk."

"Jesus, bro! Why do you have to take something fun and make it sound so . . . middle-aged? It's hardly a relationship, it's just been a couple of weeks."

"Try six."

"I like her. And if you made any effort at all, you'd see she's pretty cool. So stop bad-mouthing her."

"Rían, we need to be sure." Adam put his hand on his brother's shoulder. "Look, Meg and I have to go; we're doing the airport pick-up."

"Who's arriving?" Rían asked, scratching his head.

"Your head is so up your arse, Rían," Adam snapped. "It's Thursday! Hugh is coming down to start preparation for the alignment."

"So we have another exciting holiday ahead of us?"

"Sulking is a very unattractive trait, Rían," Áine said, sounding just like Sister Basil, the school principal. "Besides, Matthew is coming too, so you can be entertained as we put on a lovey-dovey act for Hugh."

Rían perked up. "At least there will be someone to poke fun at. But why is Matthew coming here for Easter? Doesn't he have his own family to bore senseless?"

Áine giggled and then gave him a reproving look. "He wants to make sure he's playing his part sufficiently well by showing how 'committed' he is to our relationship. I promised him I'd put on a good show."

I doubled up laughing. "The poor guy doesn't know what he's in for."

"So do you think you're ready for the alignment?" Adam asked as we pulled into the parking lot at the airport.

I shrugged. "I suppose so. You don't sound too excited."

"To be honest, I never thought it would happen. I don't know if I'll ever really be ready."

"It's what we were given these elements for. I'm sure we'll be able to pull it off."

"It's good that you're confident. I guess I've had more time to doubt myself than you have." He sighed. "Come on; Hugh should have landed by now."

We got out of the car and walked toward the terminal. Even though it was crowded, Hugh was easy to spot, looking more like Dr. Watson from Sherlock Holmes than ever.

"Adam, Megan, hello," Hugh cried with outstretched arms. He gathered me up in a bear hug.

"Hugh! It's great to see you," I said when he finally released me.

"And you too, my dear. I hope you have all been keeping well." He turned to Adam and clamped his hand down on his shoulder in a fatherly gesture.

"We're fine," Adam said. "Have you any news for us?"

Hugh frowned. "All in good time, my dear boy, all in good time. Tell me, where is the strapping young Matthew? We hear he and Áine have hit it off better than anyone could have hoped for."

Adam smirked. "Oh, they hit it off, all right. Áine can barely control her excitement at seeing him today."

When Matthew's flight arrived twenty minutes later, he loped over to us with a smile.

"Megan, hi," he said, wrapping me in a cloud of alcohol fumes.

I took in his glow. "You're looking well."

His eyes crossed for a second, and he staggered a bit. "Having a generous trust courtesy of the Order has its advantages," he stage-whispered in my ear. "I've been skiing in Austria for the past week." He must've caught the look of death Adam was giving him, because he pulled away from me and nodded in Hugh's direction. "Tweed suit, pink bow tie, and an old leather bag full of books. . . . I'm guessing you're Dublin Order?"

"You're Áine's intended?" Hugh asked. His face turned several shades of red before settling on flushed pink.

Matthew gave an exaggerated bow. "The one and only."

"Let's get you a cup of coffee before we go anywhere," Adam said, grabbing Matthew by the sleeve and dragging him away.

Hugh's eyes bulged. "*That* is what Áine is expected to marry? It can't be. He was hand-selected! We were assured, nothing but the very best would be considered for—"

"It's all right, Hugh. He's not normally like that."

Adam and Matthew, now clutching a coffee cup, rejoined us.

"Let's get going," Adam said, grasping my hand and leading the way to the parking lot. As soon as we were out of earshot of Hugh, I started talking. "He has a trust fund from the Order?"

"It's an incentive, I guess."

"He's paid to be Áine's intended? You can't be serious."

"We all know how much it sucks to have your future decided for you. I'm sure having the Order pick up all your bills is major incentive not to opt out."

"I guess so, but he'd be staying for all the wrong reasons."

Adam shrugged. "There are no right reasons when it comes to arranged pairings. It certainly isn't for love, so why not money?"

I felt my skin begin to crawl. "I thought it was more about honor and obligation."

Adam glanced at me squinting against the sun. "Once upon a time, yeah, but times have changed."

I rubbed my arms as if it would wipe away the dirty residue the conversation had left on me. "So why don't the Marked have trust funds? Surely you deserve what the intendeds get, if not more."

"We do."

"You have a trust?"

"The Order sees that we are all financially taken care of, but we don't use it."

"What?" I gasped, turning to him in surprise. "You mean, you're loaded, but you don't use the money?"

"You know how Fionn feels about the Order. He doesn't want anything from them, so he never accepted any money. We didn't have personal access to our trust funds until we turned eighteen."

"But you're eighteen now. You could spend it on anything you want!"

"We don't, out of respect for Fionn, and because we don't need it. He looks after us."

"Do *I* have one?"

"I guess."

"So you're telling me I'm rich." I stopped walking, my thoughts churning.

When Adam realized I was no longer beside him, he swung around and exhaled heavily. "Potentially, yeah, when you turn eighteen." A sly smile crept across his lips. "Until then, you're still a pauper."

"And it never occurred to you to tell me?"

"Nope. As I said, I don't think about it; it's just there. We respect Fionn's decision."

"Think of all you could do."

Adam's eyes narrowed. "Megan, the Order is a twisted organization built on centuries of corruption, betrayal, and power. Everything you take from them comes at a price. Don't let the Dublin Order lull you into a false sense of security. They're not all like that."

His words lingered in my mind through the entire ride home. There was so much I didn't know about the Order. The depth of the distrust and the scars of betrayal went far deeper than I thought.

As we got out of the car at the DeRíses', Matthew stumbled and fell against me. "You know, Áine doesn't want me."

"It's not like that, Ma—"

He shook his head. "Nope, she won't have me." His sandy hair flopped down over his crossed eyes. "You could have me . . . if she won't, you can. I can be . . ." He turned his head slightly to the side and burped. "S'cuse me." He giggled. "I can be your intended."

"Tempting," I muttered as my eyes darted to Adam. He approached Matthew with a face that could sour milk.

Áine came running out, pushed past Adam, and threw herself between Matthew and me. He looked winded for a second, then locked his arms around her, diving in for a killer, full-on kiss.

Áine fought him off. "Matthew! Not . . . in front of everyone."

Hugh smiled uncertainly. "Um, well, I'll leave you youngsters to catch up," he said, and shuffled across the yard to the scullery door.

As soon as he was out of sight, Áine shoved Matthew.

"What the hell was that?"

"I was role-playing."

"Ugh!" Áine wiped her mouth again.

Adam's hand slipped into mine. "Don't mind him, Áine. He's langers. You better sober him up before dinner—otherwise, he'll open his big fat gob."

Áine grabbed Matthew's sleeve and pulled him toward the house.

"Oh, and Matthew," Adam called after him. Matthew turned slowly, suddenly looking a little less drunk. "Stay the hell away from Megan."

Inside, Fionn was ushering Hugh down the hall to his study. "Megan, any chance you could have dinner with us tomorrow?"

"I would love that, Fionn. Thanks."

"Excellent," he said, disappearing from view.

Adam shook his head, leaned back against the kitchen table, and gazed into the hall. "I don't know what's gotten into him."

"What do you mean?"

"He's been making a big deal out of every family meal, like each one is our last. It's beginning to freak me out."

"Really? I hadn't noticed."

"That's because you don't know him like I do." Adam's troubled eyes met mine.

"There are going to be some huge changes over the

next year," I said. "Once the alignment is done, there won't be anything tying you all here anymore. You guys are all he's ever known. When you think about it, it must be fairly daunting." As I said the words, the realization hit. Áine, Adam, and Rían had their own lives to lead, loves to be found, and families to be had. Where did it all leave Fionn? I felt a sudden rush of compassion for the man who had dedicated his entire life to them . . . to us.

Adam's face softened. "I never really thought of Fionn's future or our future without him. He's always just been there."

Áine trundled down the stairs and stopped at the kitchen door. "Hey, guys, fancy going out later? I don't want Matthew talking to Hugh tonight—he could wreck everything."

"Maybe. Where is he?" Adam asked.

"Passed out on my bed. What was he thinking? He knew Hugh was going to be here!"

"Maybe you two should talk some more about this whole intended thing," I said. "He doesn't seem too happy about it."

"Nah, he's fine," Áine said.

I scrunched up my face. "Trust me, have another chat."

"Not now. The last semi-coherent thing he said was 'digia know b-b-bannnnanash wash a herb?'"

I laughed. "Oh god, he's a mess."

"So are you up for tonight?" she asked again.

"Sure, but I promised Caitlin I'd drop by."

"Bring her along as well."

I turned back to Adam. "You want to?"

"Sure."

"Okay, Áine, you're on. I'll call Caitlin."

Matthew sobered up by the evening. Looking a little sheepish and nursing a massive hangover, he came out with us and actually seemed to fall for Caitlin. The speed at which he could swap affections left me dizzy.

We went to a local pub called the White Lady. It still felt weird to me that we could all hang out in a bar. I kept expecting to be carded. Tonight there was a cool band playing, and the place was buzzing. The only thing bringing me down was Rían, who sat in the corner of our booth, looking miserable. I imagined myself running my finger over his angular profile. His eyes met mine. For a moment, I couldn't look away. A crooked smile worked its way across his face, and the bottom fell out of my stomach. What was wrong with me? I had to get a grip. I got up.

"Are you okay?" Adam asked.

"Sure, I'm just going to the bathroom," I said, avoiding his eyes. I didn't dare to breathe until I was away from everyone and standing in front of the sink. "You do not want Rían. You do not want Rían," I whispered to myself over and over as I splashed cold water on my cheeks. But all I could see were Rían's black eyes, laden with unspoken intentions.

I finally got myself under control and erased the smoldering image of his face from my brain. Relieved, I fixed my hair and opened the door. There, leaning against the wall, was Rían.

"Why are you here?" I asked, feeling my stomach start to twist again. I glanced down the little hallway, filled with crates of empty bottles and smelling of stale beer, wondering if we could be seen. Luckily, our table was hidden around the corner.

"I was just checking on you. You seemed a bit . . . shaken."

I tucked my hair behind my ears with trembling fingers. "Oh, I'm fine." I started to leave, but Rían put his arm across the narrow hall, blocking my way. I tried desperately to avoid his dark, burning eyes boring into mine.

"What are you doing?"

"No, Megan. The question is, what are *you* doing?"

"What do you mean?"

"You know what I'm talking about."

"No, I don't."

He swung around so his hands were on the wall on either side of my face. "You're not a good liar, Megan."

"Rían, please stop. Adam will see us."

He leaned closer to me. I could see my reflection in

his pupils, my face surrounded in a halo of flickering flames in his irises. His eyes held me in a vise grip.

"He'll see what?" Rían whispered, his lips now so close to mine that I could feel his breath.

"Rían, please, don't do this." I pressed my head into the wall, trying to put distance between us.

"Do what? Ignore this thing going on between us? Ignore the fact that when I'm with Chloe, I have to push images of you out of my mind? Get over the near-murderous thoughts I have toward Adam every time he touches you? Do you know how screwed up this is, Megan? Whatever you're doing, stop it."

Anger boiled up in me. "You think it's me doing this? Did it ever cross your mind that it's you? I love Adam. I'd never be with you. EVER. So get over yourself." But the thudding in my chest threatened to betray my words.

He stepped closer to me, his body brushing against mine. "I don't want you either," he growled, staring at my lips. "I don't." The words caught in his throat as his mouth dropped to mine.

"Ahem!"

Rían jumped back. His eyes darted to Caitlin, who stood tapping her foot beside us. Rían stumbled over himself and disappeared into the men's room.

I was still pressed against the wall, heart racing as my chest burned. I raised a hand to my mouth, running my fingers over the tingling skin where Rían's lips had briefly met mine.

"What are you doing?" Caitlin asked, wide-eyed with shock. She grabbed my hand and hauled me back into the bathroom.

I moaned, slithering down the wall. "I don't know what's wrong with me."

"You and Rían . . . seriously?"

"No! There is no me and Rían—I don't know what happened. He followed me out, then pinned me against the wall, we were just talking, then . . ."

"What about Adam and Chloe?"

"It was just a moment of stupidity. It will NEVER happen again."

Caitlin's eyes glazed over with disappointment. "I thought you and Adam were happy."

"We are, it's just . . ."

"Just what?" she said, sliding down the wall beside me and taking my hand. "What's wrong?"

"Seeing Chloe and Rían so . . . so physical. Maybe . . . I don't know, I think I might be a little jealous."

"And you and Adam don't . . . ?"

I shook my head. "It's complicated. But I do love him. And I don't want to be with anyone else. It's just sometimes when Rían looks at me, I get this wave of feelings . . ."

"But you've got Adam, and he's devoted to you."

"Right."

"Well, I guess we're all allowed moments of complete and utter stupidity."

I frowned. "Forgive me?"

"Hey, it's not me who needs to forgive you."

I felt my face drop.

"Don't worry, I won't say anything. But you better make sure Rían doesn't plan on opening his mouth, because if he does, you'd be wise to get to Adam first."

"You took your time," Adam said, taking my hand as I returned to the table.

"Oh, you know us girls in the loos, it's all fun, fun, fun," Caitlin said, breezily flopping into the booth beside Matthew.

I looked at Rían's stale, untouched pint on the other side of the table and noticed his jacket was gone. "Where did Rían go?"

"He suddenly had the urgent need to talk to Chloe. No doubt he's whispering sweet nothings to her at this very second." Adam laughed. My heart raced. What if Rían told Chloe? How could I have done this to them? How could I have these feelings?

"You look tired. You want to get out of here?" Adam whispered in my ear.

I nodded, relieved at the idea of putting distance between myself and the scene of the crime. I leaned into Caitlin. "Do you mind if Adam and I take off?"

Matthew perked up. "Don't worry about Caitlin. I'll make sure she gets home safe," he said in a voice laden with meaning. He put his arm around a startled-looking Caitlin.

Áine laughed. "Don't worry, Caitlin, I will see you home too. Lothario here"—she elbowed Matthew—"can ply his wares another time. Matthew, can't you see you're scaring the poor girl?"

"Aren't you two sort of an item or something?" Caitlin asked in confusion.

"No. Our families were kinda hoping we would be, so we just play along, is all," Áine reassured her.

Caitlin visibly relaxed and grinned up at me. "In that case, I'll be fine."

"Come on," Adam said, taking my hand and pulling me to the exit of the pub. "Let's go."

The evening was cold, crisp, and clear. Adam took a deep breath. "You want to go home or do you fancy a walk?"

I gazed up at the sky. "A walk sounds nice."

We wandered hand in hand through the little winding streets with Randel shadowing us. As we left the twinkling lights of town behind, we made our way along the water's edge, stepping over the crab pots and neatly folded fishing nets that dotted the quay wall all the way to the marina.

"Come on," Adam murmured. He punched in the code at the yacht-club gate and pulled me through it. The beauty of the marina at night always took my breath away. The only sounds were the tinkling music of the masts swaying gently above us, and the quiet lapping of the water as it wrapped itself seductively around the boats. Adam led me down the gangway toward the club's yacht and lifted me on board. A wave of guilt crashed over me, and I shuddered.

"Hang on, it's a bit cold." Adam ran down the stairs and came back up with a big fleece blanket. He wrapped it around both of us and hugged me close as we sat on deck. He turned to me and let his lips gently graze mine. His eyes were closed and his face peaceful.

Any lingering thoughts of Rían were pushed firmly from my mind as I gave in to the sensation of his warm caresses. I could feel the elemental energy encircle us, but it was pleasurable and gentle.

"It's a beautiful night," he whispered hoarsely into my neck.

I nodded, not daring to speak.

"You know you're my everything?"

I squeezed my eyes shut tight, leaned into him, and whispered, "I know."

I would tell him what happened, I would. But not tonight.

Eleven

UNCOVERED

I was perched on the couch in the family room between Dad and Petra with a giant bowl of popcorn on my lap. As much as Petra's presence irritated me, I was relieved Dad had insisted I stay home to spend "family time" with her. It meant I could keep my distance from Rían. I tried to focus on the explosions of the latest blockbuster as it blared on the TV, but I was acutely aware of my dad's hand holding Petra's just behind my head.

I slithered off the couch and sat cross-legged on the floor, leaving room for Petra and Dad to get closer. Dad was happy, happier than I'd seen him in . . . well, probably since Mom was alive. And despite the weirdness of our little chat a couple of weeks ago in the kitchen, Petra was okay. Sitting on the floor in the dark with Dad and Petra occupied, I began playing with the popcorn, letting my air element pick up a piece and float it to my lips. I bit at it and grinned.

Chewing slowly, I got an idea. Adam had mentioned once that he could control water temperature. If he could do it with water, then maybe I could do the same with air. I'd never tried before, but it seemed like a plausible explanation for what happened that day with the grass. Maybe I'd burned it. I raked through the popcorn, looking for a kernel, and placed one in my hand. I stared at it on my palm and willed the air around it to heat. Suddenly it burst open in my hand. I jumped a little in surprise, but neither Dad nor Petra seemed to notice. *Cool.*

I put my hand over the bowl and tried it on a grander scale. The bowl shuddered as remaining kernels popped. I laughed quietly to myself until I was tapped on the shoulder and Petra's voice whispered in my ear. "Are you finished playing with the popcorn? Mind if I have some?"

"Sure." I didn't dare look her in the eye. My mind raced. If she'd seen anything, she'd have said something, right?

The next morning, I was both reluctant and eager to get to the DeRíses'. Since I'd have to stay home on Easter Sunday to spend "quality time" with my dad and Petra, Fionn had planned a festive dinner for Saturday instead, so we could all be together. The best part should have been that Dad and Petra were going to a party and would be out late, so I was staying over. But all that time would give me the perfect opportunity to tell Adam what happened with Rían. I knew I needed to come clean, but I was dreading it. I wasn't the only uncomfortable one as we sat down to dinner. Rían sat silent, eyes cast downward. The right side of his face was puffy and purplish-black. I wanted to ask what happened, but Áine shot me a warning look and I kept my mouth shut.

Matthew, who had returned to his devoted intended role, had several helpings of dinner and washed it down with copious amounts of wine. He seemed oblivious to the undercurrents of discontent that rippled around the table.

Adam and I finally excused ourselves and left Áine and Matthew to play the happy couple for Hugh's benefit. We ventured into town, where the Easter festivities were in full swing. The sounds of music and merriment oozed from the doors of the numerous pubs that lined the main street. Ahead of us, blocking the road, a folk band entertained a huge crowd of dancing people. Adam pulled me down a small side street to avoid the chaos.

It was the opportunity I'd been waiting for. "Adam, I have to tell you something."

"What's up?" His downturned eyes flickered to mine.

"Um, I need to give you a little backstory first. I . . ."

Without warning, Adam pulled up short and tugged on my arm. "What is it?" I asked, looking around.

He put his finger to his lips and pointed across the road, where two seagulls were fighting over a discarded bag of chips. I shrugged, wondering what the big deal was. "Seagulls?"

He shook his head. "Look beyond them."

Adam pulled me behind a car and crouched down. I scrutinized the parking lot, searching for something amiss. Then I saw what had caught his attention. Chloe. I hadn't even recognized her at first. She was wearing dark glasses and a hat, and her long legs were bound in skintight jeans and black leather boots. She leaned up against a black BMW, talking to a man. A range of emotions passed through me, the strongest of which was stupidity. Adam was right—there was no way she was seventeen.

She laughed out loud and raised a gloved hand to tuck some of her hair back under her hat. She stopped laughing as her eyes focused in our direction for a moment.

"Shit," Adam whispered as we ducked down lower.

I held my breath. "Did she see us?"

Adam crept back up, looking through the window at her. "No, I don't think so."

I stretched up and watched as Chloe dropped a set of keys in the man's palm, then slid into the car. The engine purred into action, and she pulled out fast, the tinted windows blocking her from our view.

"Who is she?" I managed to say, still frozen in my crouched position.

"I have no idea. Come on. Let's stay with that guy and see where he goes." Adam helped me up, and we followed the man as he headed through the town and onto the pier road in the direction of the marina. We watched as he let himself into the apartment building across from the marina using the keys from Chloe.

Adam took his phone out of his pocket and tapped the screen. "Áine, meet me downtown. Bring Randel too. We'll be by Gallery 41 on the waterfront." He hung up and turned to me. "We need her sight."

A few minutes later, Áine arrived with Matthew and Randel in tow. "What's up?"

"We saw Chloe. It looks like she's quite the little actress. She drove out of town in a Beemer, looking closer to twenty-seven than seventeen."

Áine's face dropped. "Aww, crap."

"She gave her keys to a guy just before she left, and we followed him to that apartment block over there." Adam pointed to the door.

"You want Randel to check it out?" she asked.

Adam nodded, and Randel flew down onto the wall behind Áine. Áine closed her eyes, and Randel set off in the direction of the apartment block, landing on a windowsill high above us.

"Not that apartment," Áine mumbled. Randel jumped to the next window and then onto a balcony. "Not that one either. Hang on, go back to that one. Black hair, heavy build, brown jacket?" she asked, opening one eye in Adam's direction.

"That's him," Adam said. "Can you get a look around the apartment?"

"The blinds are closed. I can only see through a small gap in the balcony curtain."

"Can you see what he's doing?"

"He's on the phone. Wait . . . now he's getting up. Shite, he's leaving again—he's on his way down." She opened her eyes.

"Okay. Have Randel watch him from a safe distance, and ask him to check in regularly. I'm going in."

"Adam, no. It could be dangerous," I protested. "Come on, let's get out of here."

"It will be all right. You do the breaking, I'll do the entering."

"What?"

He grabbed my hand. "Matthew, keep an eye out and watch Áine's back while we're up there, okay?"

"Okay," he said, eyes gleaming.

Once we saw the man make his way down the street to the local fish-and-chip shop, Adam and I walked up to the door. "Go on, open it," Adam urged me.

"And how do you expect me to do that?"

"Use your power. Shape the air in the lock and increase the pressure—it should pop right open."

"You seriously want me to open this lock with just air?"

"Stop doubting yourself and do it." He looked over his shoulder. "And any chance you can speed it up?"

My heart pumped wildly as I put my hand over the keyhole. I closed my eyes briefly, imagining the mechanism in my head, and the lock clicked open. I caught my breath. It seemed too easy. "This feels wrong, Adam," I whispered as I followed him inside and up the stairs.

"We're just going to check it out." He turned to me and motioned to the door. "Work your magic."

I put my hand over the lock, and even easier than the last time, it clicked open. Adam walked in, but I hesitated.

"Meg," Adam called from inside. "You have got to see this."

Curious now, I stepped into the apartment. It was more like a command station than a home. The living area was set up like an office. There were boards up around the room, with photos pinned everywhere, including pictures of our friends, the school, the marina, Dad, Petra, my house, my bedroom. Two laptops were on a live feed from cameras on my house, the school, a house I didn't recognize, and the DeRíses'. Then Chloe's school uniform caught my eye, hanging on the back of the door.

"Jesus Christ!" Adam exclaimed. "I don't know what I was expecting, but it certainly wasn't this." He took out his phone and started snapping pictures.

I went to check out one of the bedrooms. It had two single beds, both of which were made and looked untouched. I headed into the other room and found a double. It too had been made, but had obviously been used recently. I opened the closet door and peeked inside. On one end were all the clothes Chloe usually wore, and on the other was a much more severe and sophisticated wardrobe. Below them were all the bags of stuff she had bought on our shopping trip. Nothing had been touched. I couldn't believe it. Who was she? What was she?

"Megan," Adam called from the sitting room. "We better get a move on." We made our way back to the door. On the table, I spotted my name in an open file and stopped to take a closer look. It seemed to be a daily account of my every movement. "Look," Adam said, leaning over me. Sitting there was an email printout, an airline booking reference for Chloe. "Chloe is off to Sweden."

Adam's phone rang, and something tapped at the window. He answered the call while I peeked out behind the curtain. Randel hammered his beak against the glass.

Adam came up behind me. "We better get out. He's on his way back up." I ran for the door. "It's too late for that," he said, grabbing the email with Chloe's flight information. His head darted from side to side, looking for an escape. "We'll have to hide."

"Come here." I led him outside to the balcony and locked the door behind us. "Hold on, I've never done this before."

"Never done what?"

"This." I threw my arms around him and leaped off

the balcony. I heard the air whistle past my ears as we fell, and my stomach fluttered for a second like I was on a roller coaster, but then the gentle wind that tossed my hair upward became viscous and formed a cushioned hold around us. Fond memories of being wrapped in a warm, soft blanket and hugged by my mother flooded my senses as my power took over. The current of air carried us slowly downward until we were planted safely on the ground. With my head still buzzing from the delight that trickled through it, I laughed. It was exhilarating.

"Impressive," Adam gasped. "I didn't know what you were up to there for a minute."

My lips curled into a smile. "I guess I have my uses. Now come on, let's get out of here."

Twelve

ENSNARED

We burst into the DeRíses' house, yelling for Fionn and Rían.

"What's going on?" Fionn demanded.

"It's Chloe," Adam said, and handed over his phone containing the photos. "Her whole apartment is a stake-out. They have a camera on our house as well as Megan's."

Fionn sighed. "Knights. I guessed as much. Hugh, get your arse down here!"

Áine gasped. "You suspected? Why didn't you say anything?"

"It made sense to go along with the charade, and I knew there was no way we could get rid of them. If we

106

acted like we didn't suspect them, they'd have to keep their distance."

"But they didn't," Áine said. "You should have told us."

Fionn narrowed his eyes. "What do you me—"

"Yes?" Hugh came out, looking a little sheepish. "What's the matter?"

"You have Knights watching us?" Fionn asked.

Hugh's eyes dropped. "The Order knew you would never allow it, so it had to be done quietly."

Fionn was still. "You keep saying we can trust you, yet you continue to deceive us. They were watching us before you even told us about the reinstatement, weren't they?"

"It was for your own benefit. The Knights and the Council insisted. Honestly, Fionn, they're different now."

"Sending in Chloe to befriend the kids was low, even for the Knights. You say it's different this time, but they're already breaking codes by getting this close."

Hugh looked confused. "The Knights aren't allowed to interact with the Marked. You must be mistaken."

Adam glared at him. "We're not mistaken. It looks like your Knights have been misbehaving."

Hugh started pulling at his bow tie. "Adam, we had no choice. The Order was going to send the Knights whether or not Fionn approved. We are starting the last stages of the alignment training. The stakes have never been higher."

Adam nodded. "I believe you, but you should have come clean with us. Rían is going to freak out."

"Freak out about what?" Rían asked, coming down the stairs and tugging his earphones out by the wire. He took in the serious atmosphere and pulled up short.

Adam handed Rían his phone with the photos of Chloe's apartment.

"What is this?"

"It's Chloe's place," Adam said quietly. "She's been staking us out this whole time. I'm so sorry, bro, but Chloe is a Knight."

Fionn watched them carefully. "Oh, for the love of god, Rían, please tell me you're not involved with her."

Rían shook his head back and forth, color draining from his face. "No, it's impossible." He turned to Fionn. "You said she was clean."

"No! What I said was to leave it with me. That was not permission to start going out with her."

"A Knight would never get involved with a Marked. It's unheard of," Hugh said, before cowering away from Fionn's withering look.

The room began to get warm, too warm. Heat was radiating from Rían. Fionn backed down, and his voice grew reassuring. "Rían, this might all be a misunderstanding. Let's not jump to conclusions just yet, okay?"

Rían held up his hand to quiet Fionn. "Not jump to conclusions? Like what, Fionn, huh? Like, let's say, being betrayed, lied to, laughed at? Oh no, it couldn't possibly be anything like that, could it? No, that bitch was just an innocent party in all of this. 'I'm going home to the UK to spend Easter with my family,'" he said, mimicking her voice. The bruised skin around his eye and the bloodshot veins gave him a sinister air as he scanned the room. His eyes stopped at mine and burned deep into me. The sensation stabbed at my element. "Where is she now?" he roared.

Adam moved forward with his hands up. "We saw her in town about an hour ago, but she was leaving. I found this," he said, handing Rían the crumpled email from his pocket.

Rían ripped it out of Adam's hand and stared down at it with murderous eyes. "She's been here in Kinsale the last few days, then." He laughed bitterly. "She must have got some kicks out of the phone calls to me, telling me all about the weather in London and how much she missed me. What a load of crap."

"You don't know that for sure," Áine said. "She seemed to genuinely care for you."

"Oh, spare me, Áine. I know when I've been suckered and made a total fool of." He turned to Adam. "I guess you were right all along."

Adam put his arm on Rían's shoulder. "This is one occasion where I really wish I weren't. I'm so sorry, honestly I am."

Rían shrugged Adam off. "So she's a Knight, and from the look of this"—he waved the email in the air—"she's flying out to Gothenburg this evening. What's the big deal with Gothenburg, Hugh?"

Hugh sighed. "It's the Trohet Natten. Allegiance Night. The Knights gather for the ceremony every year on the islands off the coast."

"Well, I don't know about the rest of you, but I'm off to Gothenburg to gate-crash this party," Rían said. "I'm sure they will be thrilled to have a Marked One among them."

"You can't," Hugh said. "It's completely closed to anyone outside of the Knights."

"Sod that. Who's with me?" Rían's eyes darted around the room.

"I am," Adam said. "And Megan will go too."

"I will?" I said, catching my breath. "Don't get me wrong, Rían, I'm all for supporting you, but I can't just head off to Sweden. What would I tell my dad?"

"Hell, if Megan's going, then so am I," Áine said.

"And me," Matthew joined in.

"Forget it!" Fionn rubbed his temples in irritation. "None of you are going anywhere."

"Yes, we are. What could possibly happen? I'd be crashing a gig of Knights whose sworn purpose in life is to protect us." Rían crossed his arms obstinately.

Fionn raised an eyebrow. "The Knights are sworn to

protect the elements within you, not you as a person. *Never* forget that!"

"Please, Fionn," Rían pleaded through gritted teeth.

"I said no!" Fionn walked closer to Rían and lowered his voice. "She's not worth it."

"Probably not, but that's my call to make." Rían squared up to Fionn, his eyes glowing. "We're not kids anymore, Fionn. I'm old enough to make my own decisions, and I'm going." Flickering sparks lit up along his arms as his elemental magic crashed against the air surrounding him. I felt each spark strike like a fisherman's line hooking me and reeling me in. The attraction at that moment was unbearable. Ensnared by the power, I found myself moving toward the cloud of fiery sparks. I gasped as the energy from each one touched my skin and seemed to soak in, leaving a warm glow where it had passed through. As if off in the distance, Adam's voice called to me. Part of me wanted to turn and reassure him I was okay, but the other part of me—the hungry part—wanted more of the power emanating from Rían.

Rían glared at me, his eyes heavy with unspoken warnings. "What the hell are you doing, Megan? Stop!"

I want to help, I tried to say, but the words didn't make it to my lips.

Fionn tried to approach us but seemed to be repelled back. "Megan, go to Adam."

Through the fog of blissful power that surged around me, and the glinting, floating embers that surrounded us, I looked at Adam and felt my heart lurch. His eyes pleaded, and he held his hand out to me, but the energy being absorbed through my skin drove my body closer to Rían.

"Go away," Rían pleaded, and shook his head, but his hand rose up in my direction.

"No," I whispered, taking his hand in mine, gasping at the surge that ran through me. I felt the flint sparks in the atmosphere wrap themselves around my wrist like a fiery rope, binding me to him. Shock finally hit me, and I snapped my hand free of Rían's.

Rían stumbled away, looking from me to his hand. "What did you do?"

As soon as I'd broken the connection, I snapped out of the fuzzy power bubble I'd been floating in. I shook my head and took in a pale and wilting Rían. "I was just trying to help."

"You, you took . . ."

"I didn't mean to . . . I . . ." My hand continued to tingle, and I glanced down. There in my palm was a little flame, burning brightly. I gasped and clenched my fist around it.

"Megan." Adam's voice was soft. I ran into his arms, ignoring the roomful of confused eyes. He lowered his mouth to my ear. "I thought it only happened when . . ."

"I thought so too," I whispered.

"Rían, come back here!" Fionn called out. I turned to see Rían escaping out the back door.

"I'll go after him," Áine called, looking at me with dark eyes before turning to follow her brother.

"Matthew, do you mind giving us some time?" Fionn asked, though it was clear from his tone that it was more of a command than a request.

"Happy to oblige," Matthew said, stumbling over himself in his haste to leave the room.

As soon as the door closed, Fionn sat back on the bench beside Hugh, running his hand over his hair. "I'm getting too old for this," he muttered, exhaling heavily. "Can someone please explain what on earth just happened?"

Adam and I stood there. I could feel the waves of disappointment, shock, and betrayal rippling from him, even though he still held me reassuringly.

"I'm not sure," I mumbled, feeling a flush of embarrassment creep up my neck and invade my face. "I felt . . . I just needed to . . . to touch." Adam bristled beside me, and his hold loosened. "I can't explain it."

Hugh started pacing nervously. "An Ciorcal Iomlán. How? It makes sense. . . ." He scratched his head, looking at the floor. "I have to get back to Dublin."

"You don't have to go anywhere," Fionn said, standing and blocking his path. "What are you talking about?"

Hugh stared at me, then dragged his eyes back to Fionn. "I can't say anything until I'm sure."

"Just tell us!" Fionn threw his hands up in exasperation.

Hugh grabbed the front of Fionn's shirt. "No, Fionn! This time, *you* wait!" He pushed Fionn back roughly and walked to the door. "Everything you need is in my notes. Stay safe, and whatever you do, don't mention this to the Order."

Before we had time to process what he'd said, he was gone.

Thirteen

CONFUSION

"Meg and I are going to my room. We need to talk," Adam announced into the silence.

My heart thumped in my chest. I followed Adam upstairs and perched on the bed next to him. I didn't need a light to see the pain etched on his face. The soft glow of the clear night was enough.

"I don't understand," Adam finally said, his eyes still cast down.

"I don't either."

"What was that?"

"I've . . . been feeling . . ." I couldn't go on. I had no idea how to explain to him the turmoil of emotions that twisted inside me.

"Have you fallen for Rían?"

"No!" The image of Rían's pale face from earlier flashed in my mind, and everything was suddenly clear. I hadn't fallen for Rían. I had fallen for his power. "I'm drawn to him, but not in the way you're thinking. I couldn't stop myself earlier, I swear."

"I thought the power thing was just you and me. I thought you only wanted mine."

"I don't want any of them, Adam. I'm not doing this on purpose. And it's not just me! Áine keeps holding my hand, and Rían tried to—"

"He told me," he said, raising his sad eyes to mine.

"He what?" I managed to say while fighting the urge to throw up. "Why didn't you say anything?"

"He asked me not to. He said it was his fault."

"I was going to tell you, I swear."

"I know you were." He dropped his head to the side and gazed out the window.

The pressure in my throat moved higher, triggering an involuntary sob. I wanted him to hold me, to comfort me, but he didn't. He just sat on the bed, looking out at the night sky. When my tears finally stopped, I looked up to see Adam lying on his side with his eyes closed. His thick, dark lashes fluttered delicately. I gently ran the back of my hand along his jaw. How could I have hurt him like this? My element was drawn in many directions, but he was all my heart wanted. I leaned down to the warm smoothness of his face and kissed him.

"You're the one I love," I whispered, as much to myself as to Adam. I got up and tiptoed to the guest bed, climbing in without bothering to undress.

Just as I was drifting into an uneasy sleep, Adam murmured, "I know."

I opened my eyes and blinked at the bright light shining in my face. It flicked away from me, and then Áine was there, Randel on her shoulder.

"Trouble in paradise?" Áine whispered, directing the flashlight toward Adam, who was still fast asleep.

"What's wrong?" I sat up, anxious.

"Rían's gone, and so is his passport."

"You don't think he went to—"

"That's exactly what I think. But he's not going to get far. The first flight out of Cork is the five fifty a.m. to Heathrow. We still have time to stop him."

"Or go with him." Adam's voice said through the dark. Suddenly the lamp on the bedside table flickered to life.

I rubbed my eyes groggily. "We can't just get up in the middle of the night and hop on a plane."

Adam jumped off the bed. "Who says?"

"My dad, for one! He'd freak out, and so would Fionn. I don't even have my passport with me."

"Aren't you sick of everyone telling you what to do? There's a whole heap of shit going on around us, and we're just sitting on our arses waiting for other people to come up with the answers!" He walked over and held down his hand to me, daring me to go with him. "I think it's about time we started creating our own destiny."

Ignoring all the voices in my head shouting at me to say no, I let him pull me up. "I think you're right."

Áine looked at her watch. "We've got exactly one hour and fifty-six minutes to pack our bags, sneak out of here, get Meg's passport from her house, and get to the airport before check-in closes. We better get a move on." Áine grabbed a backpack from the floor and threw it at Adam.

"Has anyone thought of how we're going to finance this little trip?" I asked.

"Fionn's 'emergency only' credit card and cash stash." Áine fanned herself with it. "He's going to kill me." She smiled wryly and shoved the card into her purse along with the wad of euros. Randel fluttered from Áine's shoulder onto her bag. "I'm sorry, baby, but you can't come. I need you to keep watch on Fionn for us while we're gone, okay?" Randel made a crooning noise and hopped onto the windowsill.

"Let's get out of here," Adam whispered.

When we got to my house, my stomach dropped. There was a light on in the kitchen.

"Crap!" Adam said, turning off the engine.

"Maybe somebody just left it on," I said, getting out of the car. I peeked into the kitchen and saw nothing.

Phew. I snuck inside and tiptoed up to my room. Fast as lightning, I loaded my bag, grabbed my passport, and crept back down the stairs.

"Where are you going?" Petra's voice called softly through the darkness. A lamp switched on in the sitting room.

My heart leaped to my throat as I inched backward and looked in from the hall. "Petra, what are you doing here?"

She closed her journal in front of her and started tracing her finger over the words on the cover. "I might ask you the same thing."

"I . . . I mean, we"—I pointed out to the car—"need to go somewhere. I had to get some stuff."

"Go somewhere?" She looked at her watch. "At four thirty in the morning?"

Ignoring her questions, I narrowed my eyes. "What are you doing up at four thirty?"

She picked up her cell and glanced at it. "I got an important phone call that I had to take. I didn't want to disturb your father. So where are you going?"

"Adam's brother went somewhere, and we have to get him."

She leaned forward. "Rían? Where did he go? What's wrong?"

She knows Rían? I wasn't sure which direction I should take the lie in. "He found out his girlfriend was lying to him, and he's gone after her. We have to stop him." As soon as the last word left my mouth,

I cringed. Without all the significant details surrounding our decision, it sounded crazy.

But Petra just looked at me. "That Chloe girl, right? Where?"

I dug deep for a believable destination. "To her mother's place." I bit my lip, not meeting her gaze.

Petra's eyebrows shot up, and sarcasm crept into her voice. "Her mother's place? Really?" She stood up, went to her handbag, and produced her wallet. She nodded toward the bag on my shoulder. "I take it you're not planning on being back tomorrow." She whipped out all the cash and gave it to me. "You'll need this."

"You're not going to stop me?" Was she that desperate for my approval that she'd send me off into the unknown without so much as a question?

"*Tá sé am chun an ciorcal dul iomlán.* You need to keep Rían safe and bring him home."

I hesitated, my mind racing. Why was she talking in Irish? But I didn't have time to think about that right now. "My dad! He'll kill me. I have to explain, something, write a note . . ."

"Leave your dad to me."

"But—"

"Just go. I'll cover for you."

I looked at her for another few moments, suddenly realizing I didn't know her at all.

"Go!" she said, ushering me out the door.

We bought our tickets and ran to the departure gate. Luckily, 5:15 a.m. on Easter Sunday was not prime traveling time, and the only sound was the gentle hum of a janitor polishing the floor two gates down. As we approached, Rían looked up and smiled sadly, glancing at our bags. "I guess you're not here to stop me."

"Would we be able to if we wanted?" Adam asked with a wry grin.

Rían ran a finger over his eye, which was now turning blackish blue. "Yesterday I'd have said no to that question, but today I'm not so sure."

Adam threw his bag down beside Rían. "It's just as well we're not here to stop you, then."

"Thanks, bro," Rían said, glancing up at me warily.

I gave him a wide berth and sat down across from them. Had Adam given him the black eye?

Áine tackle hugged him. "Of course we're going with you. Do you think we'd let you do this alone?"

After a very long wait in Heathrow for a connection, we finally boarded a flight to Gothenburg. By the time we took off, the lack of sleep caught up with us. I was just dozing off when Rían tapped my shoulder and leaned forward to talk to me around the side of the seat. "Thanks for coming. You didn't have to."

I looked over uneasily at Adam, but he was sleeping peacefully. "I'm so sorry about your eye."

"I had it coming." Rían put his hand on my shoulder.

"I'm a total shit of a brother." His face darkened as he looked down at his hands. "This is a strange thing going on between you and me. It's not, you know, the real deal. It's missing something, right? Sort of like lusting after a Big Mac when there's a big, juicy piece of steak on the plate beside it."

I threw my hands to my mouth and tried to muffle my laughter. "Yes, that's exactly it! I'm the Big Mac, and Chloe's the juicy steak, right?"

His eyes crinkled and he flushed a little. "Not that I'm comparing you to a Big Mac."

"Rían, being compared to a Big Mac is the least of my worries."

His eyes dropped. "I've been meaning to talk to you about something."

"What?"

"That list you mentioned a while back, the one with the names on it. Did you find out anything more about it?"

"No. Do you know something?"

He shrugged. "Not the list but maybe the names. When I was up in Dublin working with Hugh, he was researching some sort of time line, and those names were on it."

My mouth was suddenly dry. "Mine too?"

"No. If I'd seen your name, I'd have said something to you. Look, Hugh asked me to help him out but swore me to secrecy, because the Council didn't sanction his research. I didn't think anything of it until you mentioned those names."

"Do you think Hugh planted the list?"

"No. I asked him and he flipped out. He wanted to tell you about it himself this weekend, but that obviously didn't happen. It must be something important."

"So did Fionn know about Sigrid when I asked him?"

"No, Fionn doesn't know anything. At least I don't think he does. I'm sorry I kept it from you, but I honestly thought I was doing the right thing. I was sort of flattered to be asked to help. Stupid, really. I guess I'm pretty gullible. Chloe must have seen it a mile away."

"Don't be too hard on yourself. We were all fooled by her."

"Some more so than others," Rían muttered, settling back into his seat.

I nodded in agreement and closed my eyes, but I couldn't sleep. There was something bothering me. Chloe had covered her tracks so well for nearly two months, and if the Knights' reputation was to be believed, we should never have discovered them. So how had we managed to figure it all out now?

Fourteen

ORUST

We walked out of the Gothenburg airport into arctic conditions. Nothing I'd shoved into my bag last night was even remotely appropriate for this weather. "Holy crap," I stuttered.

"I'm driving," Rían said, climbing into the driver's seat of our rental car and tapping a location into the GPS.

"Where did you get that address?" Adam asked, sliding into the backseat beside me.

Rían stopped entering the details. "Let's just say the Knights aren't that tight-lipped when it comes to fire."

"You didn't!" Adam said.

"Ah, he's all right, but it might be a good time to ring

Fionn and let him know we're okay, and that there's a Knight in Chloe's bathtub in need of assistance."

"Shit." Adam shook his head and picked up his phone.

After a very one-sided conversation that had him holding the phone away from his ear, Adam hung up. "Yeah, I guess you could say we're in trouble."

My own phone hadn't rung yet, so I was assuming that whatever Petra had told Dad was doing the trick, but because she hadn't told me what the excuse was, I couldn't even check in with him. I suddenly wished I had Petra's phone number.

"So what's the story with . . . Orust?" Adam said, leaning forward and reading the destination from the GPS.

"I'm not sure. Our Knight friend wasn't *that* talkative." Rían turned onto the highway and accelerated. "I just know it's an island, and it's joined to the mainland by a bridge."

We sat quietly for the remainder of the journey. I was mesmerized by the beauty of the landscape. Even though it was April, everything was still covered in snow, and the road cut through endless forests with trees adorned in dripping icicles. Too bad we weren't in the mood for sightseeing. Adam leaned back into the seat and pulled me toward him. He wrapped his big hand around mine reassuringly. I felt a warm glow encase my heart. Adam was my juicy steak, and nothing would ever change that. I laughed a little to myself.

Adam looked down at me. "What's so funny?"

"Oh, nothing. Just thinking of food."

"Are you hungry?"

I shook my head. "Thank you."

"For what?"

"For being you."

Adam raised an eyebrow. "Are you sure you're all right?"

"I am now," I said, snuggling into his side.

Rían finally turned onto the bridge that would take us to our destination. The setting sun was a massive red blob, slowly sinking down like molten rock disappearing into the sea. The remaining light cast a rosy glow over the pretty fishing village and trickled down onto the rocks.

As soon as we hit the island, the GPS started telling us to go down roads that didn't exist, and was constantly "recalculating." Finally Rían silenced the irritating voice and pulled up to a café, where two men were talking outside with each other. He rolled down the window, stuck his head into the icy air, and asked them how to get to Räv Ihåliga. They spoke in Swedish among themselves for a moment before turning back and peering in at us. Then in American-accented perfect English, they directed us up the hill through the forests to the other side of the island. The road was narrow and banked by snow, and the land got more wooded until Rían pulled up outside a set of unassuming gates with stone pillars and a wall that snaked its way through the trees.

He turned to face me. "Adam tells me you're a dab hand at picking locks these days. Want to try your hand at that sucker?" He pointed to the huge chain and rusty lock.

"Sure," I answered, opening the door and stepping into the bitter cold. I picked up the lock and then stopped when I noticed it was already open. I shrugged and unwrapped the chain from the gate. I stretched out my arms and pushed the gates before quickly returning to the car.

We drove up a long, meandering driveway and finally arrived at a big house in a clearing. There was no sign of any cars or people.

"Are you sure you have the right address?" Adam asked Rían as we got out of the car.

"Räv Ihåliga," he said, reading a piece of paper in his hand. "This is definitely it."

"It doesn't look like there's much of a gathering going on here," Adam said, taking my hand. "Come on, let's check out the house."

"Wait for me," Áine said nervously, catching up with us and putting her arm through Adam's. "This place gives me the creeps."

An unearthly screech came from the trees. The sound sent shivers down my spine, and I gripped Adam tightly. "Was that someone screaming?"

"Foxes," Rían said, walking past us toward the front of the house. "Räv Ihåliga means 'Fox Hollow.' I'm guessing the property was named after its inhabitants."

"And you know this, how?" Adam asked.

"There's this thing called Google. You should try it sometime. Now come on. They won't bother us if we don't bother them."

The house, built mainly of timber, was surrounded on all sides by trees. The darkness shrouded its color, but the white window frames gleamed in the moonlight. Rían paced back and forth, peering inside and becoming more agitated as the realization dawned on him that we had hit a dead end. The sun had long since set, and the woods were growing more sinister with every passing minute. I tucked myself behind Adam, who was staring at his brother with concern.

"Rían, I know it's frustrating, but they're not here. Let's call Fionn and see if he can get any more information from the Dublin Order."

"They have to be here," Rían said stubbornly.

Adam threw his hands in the air and sighed, creating a cloud of steam in the cold air. Then Áine caught my eye. She was standing still, staring off into space.

"Áine, are you all right?" I moved into her line of sight, but her vision was elsewhere.

"They *are* here. I can see them. They're in a cavern or something, and the walls are dark and damp. It's lit with candles, and there are foxes. Lots of foxes."

"Can you see how to get in?" Adam asked, almost

hypnotically as if he didn't want to risk breaking the connection to her earth sight.

She turned slightly, right and left, gazing at whatever she was seeing. "There are steps cut into the stone leading up the cave walls. They're curling up. I can't see beyond that. . . ." She sniffed at the air. "It smells . . . salty, like seaweed."

"They're in the cliffs, I bet. This house backs down to the water; I saw it on the GPS. Come on." Rían turned and ran.

"Wait," Áine called out.

But Rían was gone. Áine snapped out of her earth sight and took off after him. Adam and I followed, but I struggled to keep up, losing my footing in the deep snow. Adam gestured with his hands and the path cleared, the heavy, wet snow pliable under his hands.

"Thanks," I said, lacing my fingers through his as we ran after the others. When we got to the end of the yard, it dropped sharply toward the sea. Rían was already halfway down. Áine frantically tried to catch up with him.

I put my arms around Adam, and a flutter of excitement built up in me at the delectable feelings I was about to experience. "I think we should take the easy way." We stepped off the edge and into the comfort of the delicate tendrils of air that curled around us. Slowly we glided down the cliffside, and stepped onto a ledge that was sticking out over the water below, just in front of Rían.

He looked at me wide-eyed. "How the hell did you do that?"

"Forget about that for now. Áine is trying to tell you something."

Áine came huffing and puffing down the rock edge, gasping great clouds of steam in her exertion. "Thanks a lot, Meg. Next time, will you include me in your magical elevator?" She glared at me with her hands on her hips. "Rían, what you didn't wait around to hear is that they have guards."

"We can deal with them," Rían said offhand.

"They're not human guards; they're foxes, all around the place. This is a job for me. I won't have you going in there and decimating the entire population of Orust foxes. I'll have a little chat with them. Then you're free to do what you want with the Knights, okay?"

"Okay," Rían muttered, backing down.

"Any chance of that lift now?" Áine said pointedly at me.

"I could try, but I've never done it with more than one person, so don't blame me if this ends in disaster."

"Fine, fine, just hurry up. I'm freezing, and my hair is beginning to frizz."

Squeezing my eyes shut and taking a deep breath, I grabbed Áine. Rían and Adam wrapped their arms around us, and we stepped off the edge. Trying desperately to ignore the hum of their element power around me, I focused on the feeling of flight. It was amazing and just as easy as the first time. I felt the air reach out around us, like an extension of my own arms, surrounding each of them in a cushion and guiding them down gently to safety.

"Hey, that's pretty cool," I said, landing on a large rock by a little jetty. A few yachts were anchored offshore, barely visible against the black night sky.

"I'm guessing this is what we're looking for." Adam pointed up to an arched door molded into the rock. "We could do with some light."

"Allow me," Rían said as flames ignited in his hands. His eyes glowed eerier than normal in the dark, rugged setting. He held out his hand to illuminate the door. "Megan?"

Ignoring the urge to touch him, I moved forward, holding my hand out over the lock. Áine stepped in front of me.

"All right, guys, remember," Áine instructed, taking a deep breath. "Leave the foxes to me—just keep an eye on everything else."

"Ready?" I asked her.

She nodded. I flicked my hand, and the heavy door swung open. Áine stepped into the cave, followed closely by the rest of us. Rían's eyes glowed bright and angry. Adam stood with his arms outstretched and at the ready. My feet left the ground, leaving me hovering slightly between Rían and Adam. We edged forward, waiting for Áine's signal. Then the dark cave opened into a huge room like a subterranean cathedral. The stone walls glowed with a soft yellow-orange light.

"Welcome," a loud voice reverberated around the cavern walls.

Fifteen

FRIENDS

We stared into the cavern below us. About forty Knights lined the walls, their vivid blue gowns contrasting with the gray stone and the red of the foxes. A man in the center held out his hands to us.

"Rían, Adam, Áine, and Megan, you are very welcome." He bowed his head. "Come. Let us talk as friends."

"Friends?" Rían barked. "We are not friends."

"True, Rían, but we should be. Now please, join us."

We didn't move.

"How did you know we were coming?" Adam demanded.

"Our job is to know where you are at all times. We have been tracking you since you left Ireland."

"Who are you?" Adam asked.

The man turned his head to the side and muttered to a Knight behind him. The Knight moved out from the shadows and emerged into the candlelight. It was Chloe. A bitter feeling twisted inside me.

"Please talk to us. We need to explain," she pleaded. Rían moved away from the edge and stood against the wall, the look on his face betraying his anger. I hadn't realized the depth of his feelings until just then.

"Please," Chloe said. Her velvety brown eyes met mine. They were desperate and slightly panicked.

The man in the center spoke again. "You four are the reason for our existence, and you honor us with your presence. I beg of you—join us and let us talk."

Adam peered at him. "Tell us who you are."

"I am Cú Christenson, Grand Master of the Knights."

I could see Adam's brows furrow as he studied the man.

"I look familiar to you, don't I? That's because you are very close to my brother."

Adam's mouth dropped open. "You're Fionn's brother!"

"I am."

Adam took a second to steady himself. "Fionn never mentioned he had a brother."

"Adam, please join us and we will explain everything."

Adam eyed Áine and me before we all turned to Rían, who nodded slowly. We made our way down the curving, narrow stone steps that hugged the cavern wall. The Knights' eyes followed us, a myriad of faces respectfully keeping their distance. The foxes settled down and curled themselves into comfortable sleeping positions.

"Thank you." Cú approached me, and I let him take my hands in his. "Megan, I've heard much of you and your talents. It's an honor to meet you." Then he moved to Áine and smiled warmly. "Your powers were not exaggerated. I've never seen our foxes so content."

Rían rather pointedly stepped back.

Cú registered the movement and focused on Adam. "You're so like your father. It's a privilege to finally meet you. All of you," he added, looking at Rían. "Please sit with us." He gestured in the direction of a banquet table at the back of the cavern.

We walked with him, passing Chloe where she stood in formation at the end of the line. She kept her head bowed and made no more contact. Rían's eyes never left her. As we moved toward the table, Chloe and the Knight beside her broke rank, following us, on either side of Cú. He indicated for us to sit and lowered himself at the head of the table. As soon as the four of us were seated, Chloe and the other Knight sat down, immediately followed by the rest of them.

"Some introductions are in order—proper ones, that is." Cú spoke lightly as he poured some wine into a silver goblet. He tasted it and nodded to another Knight behind him, who promptly came around and filled our glasses. "You know my daughter, Chloe. She's my second in command and self-appointed Guardian Knight to the Marked."

I took a sip and winced at the bitter contents. Ugh!

A rumble of laughter escaped from Cú. "Give it time to breathe," he suggested. "This is Sebastian Sveningson, third in command and the Knights' chief of security."

Sebastian stood and half bowed in our direction before sitting back down. He was probably in his late twenties, with a large, stocky build, and white-blond hair that fell over a somewhat unattractive face. His big blue eyes had a softness to them, like they belonged in the body of someone who had a less kick-butt job.

Adam took the lead once more. "I guess there's no point in introducing ourselves, since everyone here seems well acquainted with us."

"This is true, Adam, so let us speak. We owe you an apology. Isn't that right, Chloe?" Cú glanced to his right.

Chloe looked up sheepishly from under her long eyelashes. "Yes, we do." She met Rían's eyes before he dropped his again.

"It was unprofessional of my daughter to befriend you," Cú continued. "Our code is strict and clear; the Knights are not meant to interact with the Marked. But now is neither the time nor the place to discuss our internal affairs." Cú paused, looking at each of us in turn. "We find ourselves in the very unusual position of having all four Marked at our Trohet banquet; never before has this occurred. Regardless of how it came to be, we're all here now, so let us enjoy it."

Adam must have decided he liked Cù, as he let go of his tight grip on my hand and raised his goblet. "To our future."

"To the dawn of a new chapter in the lives of the Marked and the Knights," Cú said, clinking his goblet with Adam's.

Adam seemed encouraged by the toast. "Why hasn't Fionn ever mentioned you?"

A shadow seemed to pass over Cú's eyes. "When your parents died, Fionn cut off all communication to the Order. As a guardian, it was the right thing to do."

Adam leaned into Cú and spoke quietly for a moment. "Does Fionn know he has a niece?" He looked at Chloe, but she was sipping her wine and watching Rían.

"No. I didn't know about her myself until she was nearly eight, when her mother could no longer care for her. I raised her as a Knight. She excelled in all aspects, climbing the ranks at amazing speed, but I fear now that might have been a mistake." He raised his voice, so Chloe and Sebastian looked toward him. "She lacked female companionship growing up. It's the only excuse I can think of as to why she'd get too close to you. Again, it's not the Knights' way."

Chloe glared at him. My mind raced; something

wasn't adding up. Cú's apparent dismay over Chloe being discovered and us having followed her here didn't quite cut it. And judging from Chloe's reaction to Cú's comments, she wasn't too worried about it either. She only seemed concerned that Rían was annoyed at her.

"Enough of me and my family problems. This evening is traditionally a night of enjoyment for the Knights. Let us celebrate."

Cú stood up. "My friends," he addressed the enraptured audience. "We celebrate our Knighthoods, who we are and those we serve." He turned and looked at the DeRíses and me. "The Marked Ones sit here amongst us as our friends, as our family. Let us raise our glasses to a future that is set out before us, more luminescent now than ever before." He raised his goblet. "To honor! *För att hedra!*"

"*För att hedra!*" the Knights repeated joyfully. Chloe stood with them, but her face was drawn, and her eyes kept flicking to Rían. More Knights entered the great hall, carrying a freshly roasted full pig. A delicious smell filled the air, and my stomach growled. I usually avoided eating anything with a face still attached, but I'd make an exception tonight.

Cú turned back to us. "Enjoy the feast with us. Now we celebrate—later we will talk."

"För att hedra means 'to honor,' right?" Adam asked.

"Yes. To the Knights, honor is everything." Cú

bowed his head and reverently picked up the medallion that hung from a blue-and-black ornate ribbon around his neck. It was a fist-sized star made up of hundreds of little stars all intricately woven together. At the center was a royal blue Celtic knot, supported on each side by a golden lion. "This is the Star of the Mark. It represents a Knight's honor. When we die, it comes with us to the grave. This particular star has been in my family for generations and is the only remaining original star in existence. The rest were destroyed by the Order after the Knights were disbanded."

Adam raised his eyebrows. "I thought you said a Knight is buried with his star?"

"Only if he takes his honor to the grave. The Knight who owned this one was denied that." Cú's face hardened for a moment, and then he continued. "New stars are crafted each time a Knight completes his extensive training and five years in residence. Even then, only the very truest of our members will receive the accolade. It's an honor we take very seriously." Cú ran his finger around the edge of the gold star and placed it gently down to his chest. "So you see, you're in safe hands."

The Knights near us hovered a few feet away until Cú invited them forward. They lay platters of the most exquisite food at our table with a flourish while careful to keep their distance. I noticed the Knights serving us wore robes of lighter blue. Cú dismissed them, and they disappeared into the shadows as silently as they had come.

"Juniors," Cú explained. "They are eager to earn their colors. Only the senior ranks will remain overnight for Trohet. The rest will be back on watch and dispersing through Europe tonight."

"Why?" I asked.

"Trohet is only for the truly committed. When a Knight is ready for his colors, he comes forward to take the Test of Truth."

I leaned in. "What is that?"

"You'll see it during the ceremony. It's a test of a Knight's purity, their belief in themselves and the greater good. If there were any cause for doubt, it would be foolish to drink from the cup. Any darkness, doubt, or fear is exposed, and it leaves its mark. Once a Knight is sure that his heart is true, he is ready for Trohet. Until then, he must be patient."

I felt myself paling. "What do you mean 'leaves its mark'?"

Cú held my gaze for a moment. "Don't worry about that, Megan. It's been a long time since a Knight has failed the Test of Truth."

Cú called for another platter to be brought to the table. The foxes that were obediently snoozing in huddles around the wall perked up their heads as the plate of meat passed by. "Áine, would you mind releasing my foxes? I'm sure they would like to join in the feast."

"Oh, sorry," she said, dragging her eyes away from Chloe. She'd been staring daggers at her since we sat down. "I'd forgotten I still had them in my head." She smiled apologetically, closed her eyes, and whispered something. The foxes promptly stretched and ran to Cú's side, forming a big circle around him.

"Amazing animals, foxes," said Cú. "When the Knights disbanded, the foxes remained here at our ancestral home awaiting our return, and are as loyal now as they were to our forefathers. It's beyond understanding, really." He rubbed the heads of the adoring animals and then dispersed the platter of meat among them.

Áine smiled and looked up at Cú. "They feel compelled to be near you. It's strange for such a solitary animal. It's like they're connected by the echoes of their past."

Cú's eyes widened, and he appeared speechless for a moment. "We have much to learn from each other." Áine, unfazed by Cú's awe, went back to staring at Chloe.

I was just about to dig her in the ribs when I realized she wasn't looking at Chloe at all. Her eyes were fixed on the third in command, Sebastian, who was focused on his food.

I leaned into Áine and whispered in her ear. "Of all the times and places to start drooling over a guy!"

"I'm not drooling," she replied. "He's just so . . . I don't know, he has . . ."

"A ginormous appetite?" I offered.

"No! He's sort of beautiful; he seems so pure, clear.

Look at those eyes," she said dreamily. "I feel like I can see into his soul. And I have to admit, it's nice to finally be attracted to a guy."

"What?" I whispered back at her, still looking at Sebastian's far-from-beautiful face as he gnawed on a big bone.

"It's just that I've been feeling strangely attracted to you lately. You know . . . the hand-holding and stuff."

You're not the only one. I laughed nervously. "You are seriously weird."

I was relieved that her misplaced affections were now directed at Sebastian, but I was pretty sure she had picked the wrong guy to crush on. He was looking loyally at Cú, and I got the feeling there was no way this guy would break the Knights' "no interaction" rule.

Adam nudged me. "Cú was just saying that we should join them for Trohet and stay here tonight. He has plenty of room and would feel a lot happier if we were under his roof instead of unprotected in Gothenburg."

Rían turned slowly and let his eyes fall on Adam. They were dark and still tinged with orange. "We don't need protection. We are perfectly fine staying in a hotel." His voice was deliberately slow and pointed.

Cú glanced nervously at Chloe, then back at Rían. "Please, Rían. I know you are upset right now, and rightly so. I can explain, but it has to be in private." I looked at the three of them and felt everything clicking into place. Cú wanted Chloe's relationship with Rían to stay a secret.

Adam and Áine gave Rían pleading looks too, but each for very different reasons.

Rían stood up, pushing his chair back sharply. "This is bullshit! You guys might have bought into this love-fest, but I'm not forgetting the real reason we came here. I need some air." He stalked off toward the steps. The foxes all jumped up and watched his hasty exit with sharp eyes.

"No!" Chloe was standing up with her hands on the table. She leaned forward, her face torn. "Rían, don't go. Just let me explain." She followed him up the stone steps that hugged the wall.

Rían's glowing eyes turned to her. "Then explain," he growled.

"Not here, Rían." She angled her head away from the Knights, but I could see her mouth. "They can't know about us." Her eyes pleaded with him. "Please, just come with me. We can go up to the house."

"Why not here?" he demanded. "I'm sure everyone wants to know the full story."

Cú banged his fist on the table. His expression changed to one of outrage. "Chloe, I'm warning you as your father and as your Grand Master, end your conversation now."

"Please," she repeated to Rían, her face now deathly pale. Her almond eyes didn't blink.

Rían's glare faltered a little, and the amber glow dulled back to his usual soft green. He ran his fingers through his hair. "Oh, whatever. I don't give a toss," he spat, brushing past her and walking back down the curving stone steps to the floor level.

Chloe stared at the spot where Rían had been standing. She took a deep breath and surreptitiously wiped away the glistening path that a tear had left on her cheek.

"Thank you, Rían," Cú said, looking relieved. "After Trohet, I will explain all I can. If you can just bear with us."

We were asked to remain seated at our table while the Trohet ceremony took place. Atop the altar, a fire burned brightly. On one side was a golden chalice with intricate engravings representing the four elements; on the other, a golden plate. Each Knight put his hood up over his head and bowed toward the stone altar. Their ancient druid roots became apparent as they stretched out their hands, letting their fingertips touch each other. Silence fell as Cú threw something on the fire that made the flames grow and burn bright green. The Knights' voices rose up around the circle, and the melodic tone of their chant reverberating around the cavern gave the illusion of a different time and place.

Cú's voice rang out around us. "Our solemn oath is binding and strong. We as Knights vow allegiance to the Marked. We bind ourselves to the elements within.

We bind ourselves to duty and honor. Let the will of the spirits guide me tonight, tomorrow, and ever after. May my judgments be pure, may my thoughts be honorable." He picked up the chalice.

Áine leaned into Adam and whispered, "Is that the—"

"Cup of Truth," Adam muttered over her, his eyes focused on the golden chalice.

As Cú took a sip, a gentle light illuminated his face. He closed his eyes and raised the cup above his head, turning his face toward the cave ceiling. He then passed it to Chloe.

I wondered for a second if she would be able to drink from it. I held my breath, and my heart skipped a beat as she raised the cup to her lips. She sipped and was bathed in the same warm, golden glow. I sighed inwardly. She was pure of heart, despite the fact that she had lied to all of us. I couldn't wait to hear Cú's explanation for everything. Once the chalice had worked its way to all the Knights, Cú picked up the golden plate and held it in front of him. Four Knights lined up, each holding an offering. The first poured a small handful of earth. The second, a burning ember. The third, a goblet of water. The fourth, a handful of nothing.

As the fourth blew the contents of his empty hand onto the plate, Cú murmured, "Nourished by earth, warmed by fire, quenched by water, and enabled by air, bound are we until the circle comes full."

He ran his hand through the contents on the plate,

mixing them together, then pulled back his robe, smearing the concoction over a trinity-knot tattoo on his collarbone, just like the one on his star. "With my body I protect; with my soul I defend." Cú then stepped out of the circle.

Chloe went next. She exposed her tattoo and smeared it, all the while staring at Rían. Each of the Knights took a turn with the plate until the circle was complete again.

Cú put both hands up to his hood and lifted it away from his face. "To another successful year, my brothers. Let us celebrate."

The Knights pushed back their hoods and cheered.

Adam came up from behind me and put his arms around my waist. My stomach flipped, and warmth radiated to the rest of my body. "We'll be back under Fionn's scrutinizing eye again tomorrow, so we should make the most of tonight," I murmured.

"We will," he promised, kissing me softly.

I suddenly realized the room had gone quiet.

Cú's face was strained and serious. His eyes swept over the Knights, and then he cleared his throat. "We know of your situation, Megan and Adam. You should know the Fifth Prophecy—the foretelling of your union, and the death and destruction that will follow—is the darkest fear of the Knights."

Adam scowled. "There is nothing to indicate that Megan and I have anything to do with the Fifth

Prophecy. People weight their argument too heavily on the Scribes, which are well known to be nothing more than ancient ramblings."

Cú dropped his voice and turned away from the prying eyes of the crowd. "Personal opinions aside, it is our job as Knights to protect your elements, no matter what the consequences. Your union jeopardizes all that we strive for and exposes your elements to the darkness."

"What darkness?" Adam asked.

"We can discuss that later. It would be best not to antagonize the other Knights with too much physical contact. Others may be watching."

"Others?" Adam asked.

"People who don't necessarily have your best interests at heart. Once your element has been exposed to the darkness, even the people you hold dear can't be trusted," Cú said with a grim look on his face.

"Not even you?" Adam asked, raising an eyebrow.

"Especially not me," he said, allowing his lips to curl into a crooked smile.

Sixteen

THE KNIGHTS

"How about a nightcap before we retire for the evening?" Cú proposed as he led us into his house. "Maybe Jägermeister?" He smiled and held out a rather ominous-looking bottle. Exhausted, Áine and I both slumped down on the couch. I landed awkwardly on my phone in my pocket, and I suddenly realized I'd never turned it on after we got off the plane. Crap!

It beeped four times as it powered up. I quickly read the texts, discarding the ones informing me of Swedish networks and roaming charges, and took a deep breath when I saw two voice mails from Dad. Yikes.

"Can you ever pick up your phone? I can't believe you planned

this with Petra without me knowing! We're on the plane now. I'll call you when we land." His voice lowered. *"They're telling me to turn off my cell—I better go. Love you. Bye."*

"And you're still not picking up," he sighed. *"We're in Paris now. I can't believe I'm in Paris! How could you have kept this a secret from me? Anyway, I tried calling you at the DeRíses'. Fionn says you're out with Adam for dinner and a movie. Have fun, and call me when you get this message."*

My thoughts were jarred for a second. Petra said she'd cover for me, but taking him to Paris? Seriously?

Adam looked over at me. "Everything okay?"

I nodded, still trying to understand why Petra would do this for me.

Rían stood across the room, looking at Chloe. She walked toward him and reached out to run her hand down his bruised face, but he flinched away.

"What happened?" she whispered.

"Like you care," Rían replied.

"You know I care. I care a lot more than I wan—" Chloe stopped abruptly and turned away as Cú caught her eye.

Cú filled up a small glass of brown liquor. "Are you going to join us, Rían?"

Rían stepped farther back and leaned against the wall. "I'm fine where I am."

"Suit yourself." Cú sank into an armchair beside Chloe with a sigh. "You must have many questions for us. I'm not even sure where to begin."

Adam leaned forward. "What are you doing here? Wouldn't it make sense for you to be based in Ireland?"

Cú shrugged. "Not really. We only intervene with the Marked when absolutely necessary. Anyway, the Marked haven't always lived in Ireland. They've moved around Europe over the centuries. When the Knights were at their strongest, this was the obvious location."

Adam frowned. "So why are you intervening now?"

"The Knox were moving in on you."

"They've moved in before."

"This time, it's different."

"What did you do with them?"

"The Knox? Well, the tracker, Lyonis, was taken out simply enough," Cú said without reflection. "The rest of the Knox that were gathering when Megan was taken were chased across Europe. We got all of them, bar a few that we lost near the Sahara. We'll get them too . . . eventually."

I felt a little ill as an unwelcome memory of Adam's body lying deathly still invaded my mind. I shuffled closer to him.

Adam squeezed my hand but kept his attention on Cú. "How many of them were there?"

Chloe spoke up before Cú could answer. "About fifteen, all waiting to make their move. They were only focused on Megan. It was the most sophisticated Knox operation we've seen. Normally they grab whomever and go, but they waited, biding their time. They're up to something."

Áine sighed beside me. "Aren't they always?"

Cú shook his head. "No, this is different. They're better organized, more disciplined."

I shuddered. With so much going on in our lives, it was easy to forget the dangers of being Marked.

"I guess we should be thankful you're even more skilled than they are," Adam said quietly.

Áine shrugged. "So why disband the Knights if you're needed? And why is Fionn so against you?"

Cú looked uncomfortable. "That is a long story, spanning decades, really. The Order of the Mark and the Marked Knights were two completely separate institutions—both existing for the Marked Ones but for two very different purposes. The Order was there to guard your history, to nurture your talents, and to protect you from discovery. We, on the other hand, were there to protect the elements at all costs. In the late 1800s, many Knox had infiltrated the Order, so much so that two of the Marked were brought up in the hands of such members. The boy and girl were being twisted and molded by the Knox, exposed to their darkness. When they turned eighteen, they broke away from the Order and disappeared into Russia."

"Exposed to their darkness?" I repeated. "You said that earlier to Adam. What does that mean?"

Cú sighed. "This is something you should be taught by the Order, but their theory is that if the darkness is hidden from you, you are less likely to be affected by it. You see, like most things, there are two sides to your element, the light and the dark."

"There is darkness in us?" I asked. "Like an evil?"

Cú shook his head. "Not evil, just an opposite. It's a balance; one cannot exist without the other. You are taught to embrace the light and to use your element in a certain way, but the dark is there. It's completely necessary and maintains the balance; the two halves are what make it possible for the element to exist in you. You must remember: Your elements are the powers of a Goddess. To her, light and dark are not good and evil, they are positive and negative. Sometimes dark deeds are essential for the greater good. But only a higher power has the ability to make that call. No human, even a Marked One, should cast judgment and use their power for destruction or dark intentions. It is the darkness that the Knox foster and then use to manipulate the Marked to their side. Do not let it trouble you. I only mentioned it because we believe strong emotional responses can trigger the imbalance. That's part of the reason why relationships between Marked Ones are feared by the Order and the Knights."

"Yet you don't seem convinced," Adam said.

Cú raised an eyebrow. "Don't I? Look, everyone has a light and a dark to them. With the Marked, it's just a little more complicated because there's more at stake. But the light and the dark don't choose you—you choose them. Alrek and Sigrid made a choice. They chose the darkness."

I gasped. The fourth name on the list. "Sigrid?"

"Yes. That was the girl who was raised by the Knox."

Rían's eyes flicked to mine, then back to Cú. "What else do you know about her?"

Cú took a deep breath and plowed on. "The Order was so embarrassed by the defection that they failed to tell us until it was too late. Sigrid and Alrek were running wild through Russia, causing mayhem. The Knox had originally wanted them to be powerful enough that they could take control of the country. But Alrek and Sigrid were consumed by the darkness that they were raised to embrace. They enjoyed watching people suffer at their hands. It is said they even started the chaos on Bloody Sunday outside the Winter Palace. The Order no longer had the Amulet of Accaious, so they couldn't remove the elements, like they'd done on previous occasions. The Knights had to intervene." He paused and knocked back the remnants of his drink. "For us, the decision was simple: Sigrid and Alrek needed to be destroyed so that the elements could be passed down. But Alrek and Sigrid got word of the plan to take them out, and they decided to take out the Knights instead.

"They managed to wipe out over half of the Knights

who had gathered for the mission. My great-great-grandfather, Ruben Christenson, was stationed at an exit that wasn't clearly visible. While Alrek and Sigrid were busy massacring the main body of Knights, Ruben drew his sword and killed them both, releasing the elements. The Order has been more careful and less cocky since that time, but they never forgave the Knights for killing two Marked Ones. The Knights eventually disbanded without financial aid from the Order, and Ruben Christenson was villainized."

"Which is why Fionn is so against the Knights?" Áine asked.

"Yes. Fionn is Order through and through, and he hates that the blood of the Knights runs in him." Cú exhaled heavily. "When Emma and Stephen DeRís were killed, it became apparent that the Order had once again become unsafe. A small pocket of the Order, knowing what they were faced with, quietly reinstated the Knights in order to offer protection if it was needed."

"A small pocket," Adam repeated. "Does that mean not everyone in the Order is aware the Knights have been reinstated?"

Cú nodded. "Yes. After all, there are still many who would not support the decision."

Adam half smiled. "You said earlier that we shouldn't trust anyone, especially you. So why should we believe you now?"

"Trust and truth are two very different things. What I'm offering now is truth. Trust must be earned, and someday I hope I can do just that."

My mind raced as I glanced over at Chloe, then back at Cú. "How about a few truths, then?" I said.

Cú raised his chin to the challenge.

"You knew Chloe was involved with Rían. Why did you hide that from the Knights?"

He looked at me for a few moments, as if gathering his thoughts. "There are two answers to your question." He raised his finger in the air. "One: Interaction with the Marked is strictly forbidden. If the other Knights were to find out how close Chloe was to you all, she'd have to face a hearing, and might even lose her star." He formed a V with his fingers. "And two: I needed her to bring you here without the Order knowing or the Knights realizing Chloe was working on a different directive."

"You orchestrated this?" Rían spat, glaring at Chloe. "You planned the whole thing?"

"I wanted to tell you, but I couldn't," Chloe said, her voice cracking a little.

I reeled. My suspicions had been right. "Last night, in the parking lot, when Adam and I saw you—"

"I was waiting for you. But I couldn't let my partner know what I was up to."

"You knew we'd come?"

Chloe shook her head. "No. But I was pretty sure you'd react the way you did."

Rían glared at her. "All the phone calls when you were in the UK, they were all lies? You were in Cork all along."

"No, I was in the UK, I swear. I was waiting on my orders." Chloe moved toward him. "I hated lying to you, Rían. Please believe me."

Rían stepped forward, closing the distance between them, and his eyes flared. "And if we didn't fall for your little charade, what then? How far were you willing to take the lies?"

"We had another plan in place."

"Another plan? What was that?"

"It doesn't matter now."

Cú pushed them apart. "Chloe had to employ rather drastic measures after she defended Megan in Cork City and you all became suspicious of her. I'm sorry, Rían, but we had no other choice. Please don't take it out on her. She did it under orders with honor in her heart. And I assure you, it was a means to an end, and end it must. For good."

"Don't I get a say?" Rían demanded.

Cú went still. "Nobody gets a say. It was an illusion to serve a purpose. If you had discovered the Knights before we got you here, we'd never have had an opportunity to talk like this. The Order would never have allowed it. But now their hand is forced. We can unite, the Order and the Knights. We need to work together for what is to come."

"We can still walk away," Adam said.

"You can, Adam, but it would be unwise."

"Why?"

"Because there is so much at play here. So much you don't understand." Cú turned and looked at me. "Give me the opportunity to help you."

Áine flexed her fingers and stared at them. "Help us with what?"

"With what's to come," Cú replied.

"And what exactly is coming?" Rían asked.

Cú took a deep breath. "Destiny."

Rían laughed. "What a load of crap. We've heard it all before."

"You *think* you've heard it all before, but you haven't. Let me come back to Ireland with you. I'll explain all when the time comes."

"Why not now?" I asked.

"Because events must unfold. Intervention may change its course or delay the outcome, but the end point is inevitable."

Áine's eyes flickered. "So what's the end point? The alignment?"

Cú shrugged. "We'll only know the inevitable when it happens."

"Ugh! You're as bad as the Order," Rían said, throwing his hands in the air.

"Trust me when I say we are not."

"You just said trust had to be earned."

"And this is where I start earning it. I'm coming back to Cork with you. It's high time my brother and I had a heart-to-heart."

Seventeen

REUNION

Chloe led me upstairs to a pretty room decorated all in white with small blue and pink flowers on the bedspread and curtains. There was a pair of pajamas laid out on the bed, and a fire was crackling away in the small white fireplace.

"You knew we'd stay," I said.

"It was more like wishful thinking." Chloe turned away, not meeting my eyes. "Áine, you're in here." She pushed the door open to a room just across from mine. "Adam, Rían, you're down here." She walked to the end of the corridor and pushed two doors open. "Take your pick."

Cú stood at the top of the stairs. "Breakfast is in the dining room at seven a.m. sharp. We took the liberty of setting the alarms in your rooms. Sleep well."

Rían went into his room and slammed the door.

Adam leaned down and kissed my cheek, whispering, "See you in a few minutes."

I closed the door softly behind me and got into pajamas. I stood in front of the fire, warming my cold feet and trying to sort through everything that had happened. There was a soft tap on the door. I looked over expecting to see Adam's face, but it was Chloe.

"What do you want?" I asked.

"A chance to explain."

I glared into the flames. "I defended you. When everyone doubted you, I was the one who convinced them otherwise. Do you have any idea how stupid I feel?"

"I thought you might understand. I thought we could still be friends."

"You thought wrong," I said, glancing at her. "I trusted you, and you used that against me." I moved toward her. "I'm sick of being the weak one, the one who has to be protected."

"Trust is not a weakness, Megan. It's what makes you strong."

"Tell that to Rían. Because going on that theory, he hasn't got much strength left in him."

Her bottom lip trembled. "What I feel for Rían is real.

I . . . I just . . . if the Knights found out about him and me, I'd lose my star and my place among them."

"After your earlier display, they have to all be guessing."

She shook her head. "No! They'd never believe I'd cross that line."

"And yet you did."

"I had to. Cú told me to do everything in my power to maneuver you to where we needed you."

"You really don't care who you hurt as long as you get what you want, do you?"

"It wasn't about what I wanted. It's what's best for the Marked and for the Knights. Don't you see that?"

"All I see is a heartless liar who betrayed her friends, her boyfriend, and even her own kind."

"That's not true! What I did, I did with honor. The Cup of Truth would have exposed me if it were not the case. The Knights are my family. They're all I've known since Cú took me in. It hurts so much to lie to them, but it is for the greater good."

"So what do you want from me? Permission to toss Rían aside just because you're afraid of the consequences?"

"I thought you of all people would understand."

"Me! Every day that I'm with Adam, I'm reminded of the repercussions of us being together, but you don't see me running away."

The silence that followed was interrupted by a gentle

knock on the door. Adam popped his head in. "Are you decent?" He pulled up short when he saw Chloe.

"I was just leaving." Chloe marched out.

"What was all that about?"

"Ugh!" I covered my eyes and dropped onto the bed. "I'm officially turning into a bitch."

"That's not true . . . you've always been a bitch."

"You're hilarious."

Adam laughed. "You know you're not a bitch."

"I am. I'm a horrible person. I've hurt you and Rían, I'm lying through my teeth to my dad, taking advantage of his girlfriend, and I just told Chloe she was a coward."

Adam sat down beside me. "That's quite a list. What's this about taking advantage of your dad's girlfriend?"

"Remember how she said she'd cover for me, so I could come here? She took my dad to Paris. Paris! And he's been leaving me messages telling me what a wonderful daughter I am. I feel so horrible."

"Everything is going to be okay. Look, your dad is blissfully unaware of anything right now, so stop freaking out. As for Petra"—he gently lifted my chin, tilting my face to his—"just be thankful she seems eager to help." His finger ran along my jawline, then slowly down my neck.

"I guess."

"Driving yourself crazy isn't going to solve anything."

He pulled back the duvet and we sank in under it, listening to the sizzling of logs on the fire.

The flickering glow created a light display on the wall and Adam's face. The room was filled with the warm, nutty smell of slow-burning logs, bringing back memories of cozy Christmases with Dad, back when things were simpler. I sighed. "We're good, aren't we, Adam? I mean . . . we never really talked about what happened with Rían."

He moved his face closer to mine until our noses were touching. "We're good."

"I'm sorry," I said, letting my lips brush his.

"Don't be. In a weird way, it's given me new hope. If the elements are reacting among all of us, maybe what's going on isn't something signaling truth in a prophecy. It might just be the way they interact."

"I hadn't thought of it like that." I leaned into him and kissed him softly, but then for the first time since our tryst in the yard, I let go of my inhibitions, testing the boundaries of where I could take this. I climbed over him on my hands and knees and kissed him until we both were gasping.

He gripped my shoulders as I pushed him back. "What are you doing?" he said.

"Testing your theory." I grabbed his hands. Holding them tight, I pushed them over his head and lowered myself onto him. I met with little resistance as my lips worked over his face and shoulders. The wind whistled outside the window, and the branches of a tree thrashed against the side of the house.

Adam moaned, dropping his head back with his eyes closed. "We should stop."

Keeping my lips on him, I whispered against his skin, "No, we should keep going."

Adam's eyes opened, and he pushed himself onto his elbows. "No, we should stop."

Heat prickled over my skin as the wave of sensuality that had engulfed me slowly rippled away like a fine silk sheet slipping to the floor. "I'm so sorry, I just . . ."

Adam smirked. "Don't apologize, I'm not complaining."

"No . . . I . . ." I climbed off him, breathless and dizzy with embarrassment.

"Megan." Adam leaned forward to pull me back. "I want this too—I'm just not . . . prepared, if you know what I mean. I wasn't exactly thinking safe sex when I packed my bag this morning."

I wanted the mattress to open up and swallow me whole. "I'm not usually . . ."

He raised his eyebrows. "A deviant sex kitten?" He pulled my hands away from my face and kissed me.

I kept my eyes closed, still embarrassed.

He put his lips to my ear and whispered, "Is my Megan in there? Megan, if you can hear me, be strong.

Some wanton goddess has taken control of your body. But I will—"

I started laughing.

Adam opened his eyes wide in mock relief. "Megan! You fought off the evil temptress! You came back to me." His face suddenly softened as he dropped the act and raked his fingers through my disheveled hair, holding it back from my face. "I love you."

My hand crept up to his cheek. "I love you too."

"It's beautiful here, isn't it?" Cú said as we left for the airport the next morning. Just as we were throwing our bags into the trunk, a small fox appeared from the woods behind him. Cú crouched down onto his knees and petted the fox adoringly. "I'll be back soon, my old friend. Can you keep an eye on things?" The fox nudged him in the leg, then sat patiently and watched us getting into the car.

Without a word, Áine jumped out of the car and ran off into the woods.

"Where is she going?" Cú asked.

"Who knows," Rían replied, standing up on the step of the Jeep and leaning over the roof.

A few moments later, Áine reappeared. Her knees were covered in snow, and she had a bulge in her coat.

"What is that?" Adam asked, climbing out of the car.

"I heard him calling. He was cold." Áine unzipped her

coat. Inside, a fox cub was nestled against her sweater.

Cú pulled the baby fox up by the scruff. "He's a scrawny little fella. Looks like he's been out all night."

"He was waiting for his mother to come back, but she didn't," Áine said, taking the cub from Cú. "What should I do with him?"

Cú wiped his hands on his pants. "Put him back where you found him."

Áine rubbed the shivering cub. "But he'll die! He's frozen as it is."

"You can't intervene with wild animals, Áine. The strong survive. The weak do not. It's the law of nature."

"But don't you see? This fox cub called to me. I normally have to call to them." Áine gave Cú a cold look. "He's special."

"Your senses are just maturing. He's not special," Cú said gruffly, getting into the car. "Now, come on."

Áine stomped back toward the house, muttering to herself.

"What are you doing?" Cú shouted out after her. She didn't answer.

Adam smiled. "That's Áine. She's not going anywhere until that cub is warm and happy."

"Oh, for Christ's sake! Áine, wait!" Cú got out of the car and jogged after her.

Adam leaned against the door and crossed his arms

over his chest. "So what's the story with you and Chloe?" he asked Rían.

Rían scowled. "Nothing."

"Didn't look like nothing this morning when you were creeping out of her room."

Rían moved close to Adam. "Just keep your trap shut. If Cú finds out that we're hooking up, he'll spaz out."

"So what, you kissed and made up?"

"Look, I'm as pissed as you that we were conned into coming here, and I wouldn't trust her as far as I could chuck her, but . . ." He backed away from Adam, and grinned. "I kinda dig the good-chick-bad-chick thing she has going on."

Adam scowled and kicked the snow. "You're twisted."

"It gets better. She's coming back to Ireland with us." Rían laughed and jumped into the car.

Adam winced. "What?"

The sound of the front door closing signaled the return of Cú, followed closely by Chloe and Sebastian.

"They're coming with us?" Adam asked, glaring at Chloe and Sebastian.

Cú smiled. "Where I go, they go. Sebastian, you take the rental."

I nudged a reluctant Adam into the Jeep and gazed back at the house. "Where's Áine?"

"She'll be out in a minute," Cú said, starting the engine.

A second later, Áine ran out of the house with her bag

on her shoulder and a huge smile across her face. "He's all wrapped up warm by the fire."

Cú held his head in his hands and grimaced.

"Are you okay?" I asked.

"Just a headache, is all. Come on, let's get going."

We stepped off the plane into the cool, damp air of Ireland, so different from the icy, dry cold of Sweden. I speed-walked for the cover of the terminal, pulling Adam closely behind me. Áine dashed past us. "What's the rush?" Adam said, half laughing.

While Cú, Sebastian, and Chloe waited for the luggage, I walked through customs with the DeRíses and into the arrivals hall.

My breath caught when I saw Fionn. He stood rigid, anger etched in the lines of his face.

Without a word, Áine powered by him, heading straight for the exit.

"Áine!" Fionn called after her.

Before we could figure out what she was doing, Cú came up behind us. "Well, well, well, if it isn't the ghost of Christmas past."

Fionn swung around and gasped. "Cú? Is that you?"

"It is," Cú said, opening his arms. The two men hugged. Fionn stepped back, keeping one hand firmly on Cú's shoulder.

"What the hell are you doing here?" Fionn shook

his head in bewilderment. "I tried to track you down, but nobody in the Order knew where you were. I can't believe it." He smiled warmly. Then his eyes dulled. "Hang on. Are you with Chloe?" He dropped his arm from Cú's shoulder and looked at the rest of us with such an expression of betrayal that I had to look away.

"I have much to explain," Cú said softly.

Fionn closed his eyes as if fighting to stay in control. "Not here!" he said through his teeth. He turned and started walking to the exit.

The rest of us hurried to keep up. When we got to Fionn's car, he spun around.

"It's just as well I came in to meet you. Adam, you take Chloe and her comrade in your car. Don't take your eyes off them," he instructed.

"Fionn, it's not like that," Rían protested.

Fionn held his hand up. "I don't want to hear it. Go get your motorbike, and follow Adam. And where the hell did Áine go?"

"I'm here," Áine piped up from behind Fionn's car.

"Good. Megan, Áine, you're with me. Get in." He held the door open, and we didn't dare argue. Cú got into the front seat. Áine looked nervously over at me and squirmed.

"Áine, what is up with you?" I pulled up short when something rancid hit my nose. "Holy crap, what's that smell?"

She pulled me out of sight of Fionn and Cú, and unzipped her coat.

"He peed all over me," she whispered.

"What!" I peered into her jacket and saw two big eyes peeking out at me.

"You didn't think I'd really leave him, did you?"

"How did you get through security?" I asked, trying not to breathe through my nose.

"Do you remember that security guy who waved us through the gate, then started hitting his head and talking to himself?"

I nodded, recalling the man who had to be taken away by his colleagues after we'd cleared. "That was you? How?"

She leaned closer to me. "You know how my powers have been weak lately? Well, all that just changed in Sweden! It's like something inside me suddenly turned on. I've been able to go deeper than ever before. Megan, I'm able to tap into people now. People! Do you know what this means?"

"That you'll be able to force airport security to allow you to smuggle animals into the country for the rest of your life?"

She gave me a wry smile. "Well, yes, that . . . but so much more."

Fionn looked in his rearview mirror. "Jesus Christ! What the hell is that hideous odor?"

"Watch this," she whispered, then turned her gaze to the back of Fionn's head.

Fionn's eyes slid from the rearview mirror, and he turned up the music and burst into song. My mouth dropped open. Fionn never sang.

Cú glanced over at his brother with raised eyebrows and then back at us and his gaze darkened. "I'd know that smell anywhere."

Áine stifled a laugh and turned back to me. "The problem is, it doesn't last very long, and it leaves the person a little agitated."

"And you've figured it all out since this morning?"

Her eyes lit up. "I've been practicing."

I gasped. "You better not have been messing around with my head."

She flushed. "Of course I haven't. Oh, look, we're home."

Fionn stopped singing abruptly and blinked hard several times. "What the hell?" He glanced around the car in confusion. "What is that stench? ÁINE!" We got out of the car, Fionn still bellowing. "Áine, get that creature into a box and to a vet! If you've brought rabies into this country, you're on your own!"

Áine hesitated. "Is Matthew still here?"

"Yes, but he's out," Fionn snapped.

Adam walked over, wrinkling his nose. "What's that god-awful stench?"

Fionn shot him a killer glare that silenced him. "Everyone in the house, now."

We filed into the kitchen and sat down. Fionn stood at the head of the table, scowling at Cú. "Chloe's presence and your appearance is obviously no coincidence. I'm guessing you're involved with the Knights, and judging by the obedient lapdog you have there"—Fionn waved his hand in Sebastian's direction—"you're quite senior. How could you, Cú? Our family has struggled to clear our name for over a century. Now, thanks to you, history is set to repeat itself."

"Enough of the dramatics, Fionn. This is a bit more complicated than you think."

"How so?" Fionn asked with sarcasm. "You join the Knights, avoid contact with me, and send your personal guard not only to spy on us but, even worse, to get involved with a Marked One! Then you turn up here with *my* family by *your* side. Tell me how it's more complicated than that?"

Cú rolled his eyes. "You haven't changed at all, Fionn; you automatically think I'm up to something bad. Yes, I joined the Knights. And whether you want to admit it or not, you need us." He paused and took a deep breath. "And Chloe is not my personal guard; she is my daughter."

"What?" Fionn's piercing gaze flicked back and forth between Chloe and Cú.

"Listen." Cú leaned forward, resting his arms on the table. "We need to talk alone."

Fionn eyed us, then flicked his head in the direction of the door. We all got up, even Chloe and Sebastian, and walked out to the yard.

We glanced at each other, all at a loss. Inside, the voices were rising.

"You're the goddamn Grand Master of the Knights?"

Ouch. This was not going to be good.

Eighteen

SPARRING

It turned out I shouldn't have worried about facing my dad. He tackle-hugged me as soon as he came in, then pulled a T-shirt and a pair of Eiffel Tower earrings from his bag.

"Thanks, Dad!" I went to put on the earrings and glanced up at Petra, who was standing behind him.

Her eyes held mine for a moment. "Right, well, I'll get that kettle on. I'm parched."

Dad zipped the suitcase back up. "I'll just put this upstairs."

"Sure, Dad." I watched as Petra laid out mugs and tea

bags. As soon as my dad was out of earshot, I rushed over to her. "Paris?"

Her steely gray eyes flickered from my face to the kitchen door. "Now is not the time to talk about this. Your father will hear."

"But *Paris*? Why did you do that?"

She shrugged and went back to making the tea. "You needed a cover story, and your dad had always wanted to go. It seemed like a good idea."

"And you did that all for me? Don't get me wrong, I appreciate it, but you don't have to buy your way into this family with grand gestures."

A laugh caught in the back of her throat. "You think I'm trying to buy your approval?"

A stillness settled on me. "If this isn't about seeking my approval, then why do it?"

"You needed to go after Rían—I enabled that. You should be thankful."

"I am, but I don't like lying to my dad."

She eased herself into the chair at the head of the table. "I don't like lies all that much either, but sometimes they're a simple fact of life. Kind of like secrets. Nobody likes secrets, but life is all about keeping them, isn't it, Megan?"

My heart skipped a beat.

She leaned forward. "So here's the deal. I'm moving in, and we'll keep each other's secrets."

Did she know enough of my secrets to use them as a threat? The sound of Dad's feet on the stairs signaled the return of Petra's smile and happy eyes, like she'd just flipped a switch.

Dad clapped his hands together as he walked in and sat beside her. "Now, where's that cup of tea?"

"Right here, just the way you like it," Petra replied.

Dad tapped the chair next to him. "Come on, Megan, I want to hear all about your weekend."

Petra's eyes met mine. "Actually, I was just telling Megan that we had decided to move in together."

Dad suddenly looked uncomfortable. "Ah, Petra, I wanted to talk to Me—"

Petra clasped my dad's hands in a reassuring way and gave him a dazzling smile. "It's okay. Megan thinks it's a wonderful idea, don't you, Meg?"

I couldn't speak. What had just happened? I couldn't let Dad move in with this conniving, manipulative cow. But if I said something, she'd tell Dad about the last two days, and I'd be grounded forever. As fear mingled with my anger, I recalled her comment about secrets and the look in her eye. I got a nauseating feeling that she knew more about me than I cared to admit. But my Mark didn't seem to think she was a threat, and the Sidhe hadn't shown up. Maybe I was blowing this completely out of proportion. Maybe I'd just encountered the queen of man hunters, determined to

176

get what she'd set her sights on. *Okay, Petra, I accept your challenge, but you won't win this game. No way. You will not hurt my dad.*

I wrapped my arms around his shoulders, breathing in the comforting, warm, soapy smell of his neck. Fighting back the sting of tears, I hugged him tight and lied through my teeth.

"Of course, Dad. I'm so happy for you."

As soon as Petra's moving in was settled, she started hauling boxes over to our place. I couldn't walk into any room without tripping over her stuff, so I decided to spend as much time as possible at Adam's house, which was fairly crowded with Matthew, Cú, and Sebastian all staying there. It was comforting to have a little army watching out for us, though Fionn was quick to remind everyone it wasn't us they were loyal to—it was our elements. Despite his reservations, Fionn looked more content than I'd ever seen him. He and Cú spent two days talking about old times over cups of tea, sitting on upturned buckets in the yard. Today, however, they'd gone up to Dublin to try to track down Hugh, who seemed to have disappeared off the face of the planet. It had been nearly a week since he'd left, and we'd heard nothing from him.

In the DeRíses' kitchen, Áine sat at the table jabbering away while Sebastian stared at the wall with a glazed expression. He'd been left behind to watch over us. He'd also—rather gallantly, I thought—offered himself up to Áine to practice her new power on, after Matthew gave her a resounding "NO," and abandoned her in favor of Caitlin. Poor Sebastian had already suffered through two days of Áine rummaging around his mind as she tried to figure out what she could do. So far, she could influence people's choices and distract their attention, but she couldn't read their minds, and this bugged her. Giving up, she'd resorted to her more traditional methods of extracting information, talking Sebastian into submission.

He dropped his head to the table and tapped his forehead on the wood. "I think I prefer it when she's messing with my brain."

Undeterred, Áine plowed on. I had to hand it to the girl—she was chock-full of persistence.

"Resistance is futile," Adam said in a robotic voice, and tapped Sebastian on the shoulder as he pulled me upstairs to his room, where I immediately flopped onto the bed.

"Are we practicing today?"

"Yes, as soon as Rían and Chloe get back." It was hard to believe, but instead of falling apart, Chloe and Rían's relationship had gotten even more intense.

"Any news from Dublin?"

Adam shook his head. "Not really. M.J. and Will said

that Hugh showed up there after he left Cork and was blathering on about circles or something, then disappeared. They haven't seen him since. It's so strange of him to abandon us in the final stages of the alignment training. I'm actually really worried."

"What about Hugh's research that Rían was working on? Did Fionn and Cú locate it?"

"Yes, what was left of it, anyway. Hugh's desk was trashed, and half his files were missing."

"And M.J. and Will aren't concerned?"

"I get the distinct impression that M.J. and Will are more anxious than they're letting on. They said they'll give him another week, but after that, they're bringing in the Order."

I lay on the bed with an uneasy feeling stirring in my stomach. "Circles," I whispered. It sounded familiar, but I couldn't place it. "Are circles mentioned in the Scribes or something?"

"Not that I'm aware of. The only circles I see are the ones that we're running in, trying to figure out all the rubbish surrounding us." He laughed softly and dropped his lips to mine. I smiled against him and wrapped my arms around his neck, kissing him back. I felt the energy flow through us, twisting and turning, gliding over our skin. It moved like a molten substance, a mixture of air and water only visible when the light hit it a certain way. Ever since Adam

179

had stopped fighting it, I'd been able to manipulate it, like a snake charmer controlling a python. I couldn't take my eyes off it or I'd lose the control. But the point was: I had control.

A thud at the window snapped us out of our magical stupor. Pushing Adam's element back to him, I glanced over and saw Randel perched outside.

"What do you want, Randel?" Adam asked, unwrapping himself from my embrace. He walked over, pulled up the old sash window, and stuck out his head.

"Time to work, lover boy." Rían's voice floated up from the yard.

"We'll be down in a sec."

While the alignment could technically be done anywhere, the Order was planning on using a place called the Hill of Tara in County Meath. I'd never been but couldn't wait to see it. Apparently it was a huge mound of echoed land that the original druids had built for the sole purpose of alignment. The hill was surrounded by the burial chambers and tombs of generations of Order and Marked dating back to the time of Danu herself.

For the alignment to work, we had to stand ten feet apart, release our elements, and let them merge with each other at the exact time when the sun was at its highest during the solstice. With our constant practicing since February, we had finally gotten to the point where we were ready for the next stage: We could release our powers, then manipulate and hold them. But as we grew in strength, so did the elements' desire to merge, and we needed Hugh back to go any further. If we merged our elements prematurely, we could inadvertently trigger an unbalanced alignment, which apparently would do more harm than good.

Without him, we were in a holding pattern. We followed our old training schedule, standing in a circle with our fingers stretched to one another, channeling our power through our hands to the person on either side of us. The elements reflected each person's strengths. It was strange to feel Áine's sweet, pleasant essence hanging gently in the air beside Adam's passionate one. Rían's courage, intensity, and overwhelming sense of protection surrounded me. I wondered what my essence felt like to them.

With no one to watch us, we worked a little longer and harder, flexing the elements to their limits without releasing them. The session started out as normal, but when I began feeling overwhelmed, I opened my eyes and gasped. My body was hovering slightly off the ground as the wind enveloped me. Across the way, flames encircled Rían, and I could see he was clenching his teeth, a deep frown etched into his brow. On my right, Áine's normally poker-straight, shoulder-length hair was caught in a static web as the nearby grass and roots grew at an amazing pace and wrapped themselves around her. Tears were falling down her pale cheeks. I dared to glance over at Adam. He too stood still, a mass of swirling clouds snaking around him. His eyes were clamped shut, and pain was engraved into his face. Why was this affecting them so?

My eyes widened as the other elements suddenly took on form and came swirling toward me, like earlier when Adam's element and mine had combined to create a molten body. Now I watched as water, fire, and earth merged into an intricate network of glowing ribbons of energy, undulating through the air. They were about to merge!

I gasped in horror. "Adam, we've got to stop! They're merging. We've gone too far!"

Adam looked at me, his eyes unfocused, glowing black and swirling blue. "What?"

"Don't you see them?"

"See what?" he asked, looking confused.

"The elements!" I pulled back, away from the radiant, viscous powers.

Adam broke the circle and faced me. With a strange mix of relief and loss, I watched all the elemental powers retract and recoil back to their owners.

I dropped my arms to my side and pulled my element deep into its hiding place inside my chest. With the bond severed, Áine collapsed to the ground. Rían stumbled forward with a groan, and Adam wavered where he stood.

"Did you guys see that?" I gasped.

Áine shook her head. "See what? I was too busy trying to stay conscious. Are you not whacked?"

I moved over to Adam, who still wobbled on his feet. "No, I feel fine." I wrapped my arms around Adam and encouraged him to lean onto me. "The elements took form, real form. They . . . they were coming after me."

"Yeah, even the elements find you irresistible." Rían laughed from where he sat cross-legged on the grass.

"Shut up, Rían!" Adam said with a slight edge. "Don't worry, Megan. The alignment must affect everyone differently. This is probably only a taste of what's to come." He finally gave up and folded down onto the grass.

Áine's head popped up. "Way to go with your inspirational speeches, Adam. I can't wait."

"Yay," Rían muttered, and flopped back onto the grass.

I sat down beside Adam as they all recovered, guilt eating at me for feeling so vital and empowered.

Adam dropped his head into my lap. "How do you do that?"

"Do what?"

"Stay strong. Look at us." He motioned toward Rían and Áine, slumped on the grass. "Why isn't this affecting you?"

"I don't know," I said, chewing on my bottom lip.

"I wish I did. Maybe during the real thing it won't be like that."

Twenty minutes later, they started to come around. Rían was first to recover. He stood up. "Want to try something that sucks a little less?"

Adam lifted his head. "That depends."

"Hang on a sec." Rían disappeared into the house and came back with Chloe in tow. "Chloe's been showing me other ways we can use the elements."

I felt the usual wave of betrayal wash over me as she drew closer. "She's not allowed here while we practice."

Rían held up a hand. "This isn't about alignment practice."

"What do you mean?" Áine asked.

"Watch this," he said, laughing. He pulled his sweater over his head, revealing a taut stomach.

I quickly averted my eyes.

Rían winked at Chloe. "Go easy on me—I'm still wiped out from practice." They started sparring. Chloe moved fast, throwing a flying kick at Rían's chest. He blocked it with a quick swipe of his arm—not with his actual arm but with fire that mimicked his movement. Next Chloe came at him with a right hook. Again, Rían blocked it with a ball of fire, as if it were solid and not flame without form.

"Ouch!" Chloe fell to her knees and cradled her hand to her chest.

"Oh shit, sorry, Chloe." Rían ran and dropped beside her, but before he could inspect her hand, a flicker of a smile crossed Chloe's face. In the next instant, she kicked her leg out under his, and he landed on his backside. She straddled him with her knees on either side of his face and held his arms above his head.

"Gotcha!" she exclaimed, grinning down at him.

Rían smiled. "You sure do."

Adam groaned.

"Pretty cool, huh?" Rían said, sitting up as Chloe rolled off him.

"How did you make it a solid, so it didn't burn her?" Áine clambered over to Chloe and inspected her hands. "She hasn't a mark!"

Rían's face lit up. "It's all about realizing the element is power. We control that power, so we can dictate the physical form it takes. You just have to want it bad enough."

"Chloe, hit me!" Áine ordered, dancing from foot to foot.

"Whoa there, Rocky, I'm not going to hit you." Chloe laughed, getting up from the ground.

"Rían, you hit me, then," Áine demanded.

"You want me to hit you?"

"Yes! Go on. Hit me!"

"Promise not to sic your rabid mutt on me?"

"Just do it!" Áine said, crouched and ready to spring.

Rían lightly punched her on the arm.

"Ow! That hurt," she squealed.

"Well, you told me to."

"Yeah, but I thought I'd be able to stop you."

"It takes practice." Rían smirked and glanced over at Chloe.

"Fionn will freak if he finds out you've been using the elements like this," Adam snapped.

"We should be prepared to defend ourselves. And what better way than with our elements?"

"But we're not allowed," Adam continued.

Rían shrugged. "We're all breaking the rules anyway. You and Megan, me and Chloe."

"Hey, I'm not breaking any rules!" Áine said, sticking her nose in the air.

"Need I remind you that you have a smuggled fox cub by the name of Sven living in your bedroom? Oh, and the fact that you've been screwing with people's heads?" Rían said, raising an eyebrow.

"No," Áine muttered, crossing her arms.

"We've all broken so many rules—why not a few more? It makes sense to be able to defend ourselves."

Adam nodded. "I guess you have a point."

Chloe stepped forward. "I can give you the technique, and you can hone your skills."

I glared at Chloe. I still didn't understand how Rían could forgive her for lying. "Isn't that what you're here for, Chloe? To protect us?"

She looked at me with guarded eyes. "I can't be with you all round the clock. A time will come when you'll need to defend yourselves. You should start now."

"Count me out. I want no part of this." I turned on my heel and started back toward the house.

Nineteen

SECRETS

On Saturday, Adam and I went for an early-morning walk on the beach. Everything that had happened over the past two weeks had left me feeling like the world was caving in on me, like the walls were edging closer, leaving me with little air to breathe. Now the fresh sea air really cleared my head. By the time we got back to the DeRíses', I was feeling good.

Áine was on her way out as we came in.

"Where are you off to?" Adam asked.

"Down to the town to do a smidgen of training." She winked and tapped the side of her head. "Seb's mind is growing resistant, and none of you will let me practice on you."

Adam exhaled heavily. "You can't just randomly pick strangers and mess with their brains. You know how it affects people."

She looked slightly deflated. "This is the coolest thing that's ever happened to me. I just want to . . . flex it a bit."

I reached out and grabbed her hand as she was leaving, surprised to find myself enjoying the fizzing sensation that used to feel uncomfortable. "Áine, it's not right."

She shrugged. "I'll be gentle, I promise. I'm getting better."

I glanced down and tried to pry my fingers open, but couldn't.

"And you say I'm weird!" Áine muttered, pulling her hand out of mine. She walked into the courtyard, where Randel soared above her in the wispy low-lying clouds of the damp morning.

"Fionn will have to rein her in," Adam said, heading into the kitchen. "She's too cavalier about the whole thing."

We each grabbed a coffee and went to hang out in his room. Shrieking laughter came from the next bedroom.

I scrunched up my face. "Let's go downstairs. I'm not listening to that."

"No! With Sebastian and Matthew lurking constantly, this is the only private place I have. I'm not being driven out of my own room by Chloe and Rían's antics." Adam scowled and banged on the wall. "I can't wait for Fionn to get home. They've been at it like rabbits since yesterday."

The noise died down, followed by some giggling. I did my best to ignore it, but hatred for Chloe washed over me. Unlike the others, I couldn't get over her betrayal. But deep down under the layers of my disapproval, I knew that jealousy fed my dislike of her. Because she had Rían. And I hated myself for feeling that way.

Adam chatted away like nothing was going on, but I couldn't focus on what he was saying. Next door, Chloe shrieked again and the muffles got louder. I drained my cup, scorching my throat in an attempt to finish it. "I'm going to get another coffee—want one?"

Adam went to stand. "I'll go."

I stopped him. "No! I'll get them."

Adam's eyes slid to the hideous orange-flowered wallpaper that divided his room from the debauchery going on next door, and he smiled wryly. "Sure, okay."

Downstairs, I flicked the kettle on, thankful to be away from the torturous sounds of Chloe and Rían. I glanced down at the papers on the counter. They were Hugh's instructions for the alignment training, written in his round, tidy script, complete with diagrams. I reached out to pick them up and knocked Adam's coffee cup over in the process, spilling the remains all over them.

"Oh crap!" I grabbed the notes and tried to shake the liquid off, but it didn't work. They were stained and soggy. I just had to hope they'd be legible when they were dry. Very carefully, I peeled away each page and lined them up on the counter where the sun streamed in. Then some unfamiliar scribbles written faintly across one of the pages caught my eye. I picked it up and held it to the sun. Behind Hugh's neat, round writing was more text indented into the thick paper. The coffee had been absorbed into the letters, but not so much where it was indented, making the older writing stand out when held against the light. The words "Ciorcal na Fírinne" jumped from the page. I didn't speak Irish but had heard enough around school. "Ciorcal" was circle. What did "na Fírinne" mean? There were symbols too, curling Celtic circles, and other words I couldn't make out. I turned the page over and could almost make out a ten-digit number on the other side. Before anything else could go wrong, I grabbed a pen and wrote down the numbers and words that were legible. "Ciorcal" kept haunting me. Hugh had said those words when I'd absorbed some of Rían's element. The night he'd walked out. I was sure I'd seen it somewhere else too. It had to all be connected.

Adam walked into the kitchen and found me peering at the backs of coffee-stained sheets of paper. "So what's on those pages that is more interesting than your boyfriend lying on his bed waiting for you?"

"Look," I said, pointing to the word "Ciorcal."

Adam squinted at the page. "I just see Hugh's handwriting."

"No, beneath it. Look at the indentations." I ran my finger along the line.

"Ciorcal na Fírinne," Adam said in beautiful-sounding Irish. "Circle of Truth."

"What's the Circle of Truth?"

He frowned. "I have no idea. Here, let me see that." Adam took the pages and held them out in front of him, allowing the sun to shine through. "This is hard to make out, but I see 'imolán.' I think that means 'whole' or 'full.'"

"Do you think this has something to do with what Hugh was going on about?"

"It could be."

"There's more. If you look at it from behind, you can just make out what looks like a cell number."

Adam sat down on the bench behind him, squinting at the page. "The Circle of Truth. That sort of sounds like . . . hang on a sec." He ran out of the kitchen and was back two minutes later, carrying one of the books from Fionn's study. "Do you see that symbol there, the three curling swirls?" He pointed to what looked like some casual scribble of Hugh's. "Look at this." He opened the book and flipped through the pages until he found what he was looking for. "The two gifts from Danu! The Amulet of Accaious and the Cup of Truth. Look at the engraving on the cup!"

I peered closer at the picture in the book, then back at

Hugh's drawings. They were the same markings. "What do the Cup of Truth and Circle of Truth have to do with each other?"

"I wonder if we'll find out when we call that mobile," Adam said, tapping the number I'd scrawled down. "Go get Rían—he needs to see this."

My legs like lead, I climbed the stairs and paused for a brief moment outside Rían's room before lightly knocking. The laughter inside came to an abrupt stop, followed by a thud, then footsteps.

The door opened a few inches, and Rían's face appeared. "What's up?"

Trying to focus on the door frame, I cleared my throat. "Adam wants you downstairs. We found something you need to see."

Rían swung the door wide. "What is it?"

I could barely think, let alone form words, as Rían grabbed his jeans and pulled them up over his boxers. "Are you all right?" he asked, putting a gentle hand on my arm as he passed by.

"I'm fine," I mumbled.

Rían made his way down the stairs, but not before glancing at me curiously. As soon as he was gone, I slumped against the banister and banged the back of my head on the wall. I had to get a grip.

"He feels the same, you know." Chloe's voice came from the room.

Crap. I turned around to face her. "I don't know what you're talking about."

"Yes, you do." She pulled on a sweater and tied up her tussled hair. "I know you hate me. I can live with that. But what I can't deal with is knowing that the guy I'm with wishes he was with someone else."

I swallowed hard, not knowing what to say.

"I see the look in your eye when Rían's around. I know what you're thinking. I certainly know what he's thinking when he sees you."

"Chloe, I don't hate you. I . . . I just, I find it hard to forgive you."

"And it has nothing to do with the fact that Rían and I are together?" She walked right up to me, her face too close for comfort.

I dropped my gaze.

"Thought as much."

"It's not like that, Chloe. Rían and I are attracted to each other, but it's our elements. Their pull is incredibly hard to resist. But we're trying."

She stepped closer and lined her mouth up with my ear. "Don't take him away from me."

I drew a sharp breath, staggered that Chloe thought I was capable of doing something so horrific. "I love Adam. I would never . . . anyway, I didn't think you even cared."

She shook her head. "I care, way more than I should. You can't imagine the ache in my heart when he wakes up in the morning and rolls over to hug me, only to look disappointed."

I softened a little, but I couldn't bring myself to offer her comfort. "You chose the Knights over Rían."

"I made that choice because of how I feel for Rían. You've no idea of the obligations I'm under. I have to see this through; it's the only way."

"We all have choices to make. If you really cared for him, you would have picked him."

She laughed sadly. "You don't get it. We don't have choices, Megan. You, me, Rían, all of us, our choices are made for us. We're following a path that's already been plotted out. You still believe they're your decisions, but you'll learn."

Her eyes searched mine for a moment before she brushed past and stood at the top of the stairs. "Look, I don't need you to forgive me, or be my friend, but please, leave me him." She trundled down the stairs without looking back.

My heart ached for the girl who loved the boy, and the boy caught in the confusion, but she'd stirred something else in my heart. Doubt.

In the kitchen, Adam and Rían had stuck the pages to the windows. Avoiding Rían's bare torso, I went to the other side of Adam. "Where's Chloe?"

Rían stared at the pages. "She's gone to get Áine and Sebastian. We've got to ring this number."

"Let's wait until the others get back." Adam glanced sideways at Rían. "And put some clothes on, for Christ's sake."

"Jealous?" Rían swung his arm up into a bodybuilding pose and laughed as he left the room.

The back door opened. I expected to see Áine, Chloe, and Sebastian coming in, but instead it was Matthew and Caitlin.

"Hey! What are you guys doing here?" I asked as Adam surreptitiously took the pages down from the window and stacked them on the counter behind him.

Matthew flushed and let go of Caitlin's hand. "We were kinda hoping we could watch a movie or something. Do you mind?"

Adam raised his eyebrows. "Sure, whatever. But as soon as Fionn gets back, you're going to have to tone this down."

Matthew smiled broadly. "Sure. I'm going home tomorrow, anyway."

Caitlin looked at him with her practiced puppy-dog eyes.

Matthew took Caitlin's sad face in his hands. "Oh, Caitie, I'll be back in a few weeks, I promise."

"Caitie?" I mouthed at Caitlin, hiding my silent guffaw from Matthew. Caitlin gave me a sly kick and hooked her arm through Matthew's.

"Eh, guys, the sitting room is that way," Adam said, pointing to the hall. "Take as much time as you need."

Caitlin skipped ahead, winking at me as she passed.

Adam scowled. "I don't like Caitlin being with him."

I laughed. "Why not? They seem like a good match."

"This is all a game to him. He's using her."

"Caitlin has her head screwed on. She knows he's leaving."

"Yeah, but he's too old for her. And he's a player. You should talk to her."

I put my arms around Adam and hugged him as tight as I could. Burying my face into his neck, I breathed in the smell of his warm skin. I think I loved him more in that moment than I ever had. "I'll talk with her tomorrow. Promise."

"Good."

Rían wandered back into the kitchen, this time fully dressed. "Come on, let's call this number. Maybe we'll be able to track down Hugh."

"I don't think you should," Chloe said, coming in the door with Áine and Sebastian. "I think we should leave this all alone. Cú will be back tomorrow. Let him handle it."

Adam glared at her. "Do you know something you're not telling us?"

Chloe shook her head. "What if someone is looking for you? Your number will lead them right back here."

"Rubbish. It was a number that Hugh had. I'm dialing it."

Chloe threw her iPhone on the table. "At least use my phone so it can't be traced back to you."

Adam dialed the number and hit the speaker key while we all waited anxiously. It rang three times before a female voice answered the phone with a curt "Hello."

I held my breath, waiting for someone to say something, but no one did. We all looked at each other. Chloe rolled her eyes and stepped forward. "Hi. We're sorry to bother you, but we were wondering if there was a Hugh at this number?"

Silence hung on the other end of the line for a few moments.

"I think you have the wrong number."

I stood stock-still. I knew that voice. My eyes met Adam's in a horrified glare.

Caitlin walked into the room talking. "Megan, does Adam have any crisps or—"

Rían grabbed her around the waist and put his hand over her mouth, while Adam dove for the end-call button. I wasn't sure who got silenced first, Caitlin or the cell.

Caitlin mumbled something through Rían's fingers and tugged his hand off her face. "What on earth is going on?" she gasped. "Why am I being manhandled by Rían?" She turned her eyes to him and smiled a bewitching smile. "Not that I'm complaining or anything."

"Who was that?" Chloe asked, looking from me to Adam.

I picked the cell off the table and stared at it. "It was Petra."

"Petra?" Sebastian asked.

"The woman who just moved into my house."

Twenty

HATE

Caitlin glanced around at our startled faces. "Am I missing something here? Why did you just hang up on Petra?"

I sat down on the bench, stunned. Petra was using Dad to get to me. I scowled at Chloe. "She's a Knight, isn't she? You've been watching us longer than you've let on, haven't you?"

Chloe took a step backward but held my eye. "I don't know what you're talking about, Megan."

Wind blew through the kitchen and whipped Hugh's instructions from the counter, tossing them around the room. The doors slammed shut as my hair twisted upward.

"Áine, get Caitlin out of here." Adam perched next to me and gripped my shoulders.

"What's going on?" Caitlin demanded. But Áine was already dragging her away.

Anger flared inside me. "You might have been able to screw with me, but nobody screws with my father. Do you have any idea how long it's been since he's been with someone? Do you?" I strained against Adam's hold on me.

Chloe backed up against the wall. "Megan, I swear, she's not a Knight."

Rían moved between Chloe and me, putting his arms up protectively. "Megan, you've got to calm down."

"I don't want to calm down!" I shouted. "She's been going out with my dad for months. He loves her. And it's all been a game!"

Sebastian edged forward. "Petra is not one of us."

Power twisted and stabbed my chest, sparking in front of my eyes. I blinked hard, trying to see through the blur of the element obstructing my view, trying to fight the urge to unleash its strength on Chloe.

"Listen to them, Megan," Adam whispered into my ear. "Petra's been living in Kinsale for years. Long before you arrived. It wouldn't make sense."

I struggled for control, focusing on my breathing and the grounding sensation of Adam's hands on my shoulders. Uncomfortable silence filtered through the thudding pulse that continued to hammer inside my skull. "So if she's not a Knight, who is she working for?"

Rían started collecting Hugh's pages from where they were scattered around the kitchen. "My guess is Order."

"Really?" Chloe asked.

"Who else could she be with?" Rían said as he sat down beside her. "She can't be Knox. We would've sensed danger from her if she was."

Adam shook his head behind me. "Something doesn't make sense. If she was Order, she wouldn't have been keeping her nose out of our business. I hadn't even heard of her until Megan moved here."

Rían scratched his jaw. "Well, if she's not Order, Knights, or Knox, then who the hell is she?"

Blood still pounded through my head, beating against my skull from the inside. I winced, wishing the pain would stop. Then, like someone had flicked on a flashlight in the darkness, I was standing in my sitting room at four thirty a.m., speaking with Petra. "I got an important phone call I had to take," she'd said. Hugh had called her! Suddenly I knew where I'd heard the circle thing before.

"An Ciorcal Iomlán," I said, cutting across their theories. "Hugh said it, the night he left, before he disappeared. Petra said it too." I shook my head. "When I got back to my house the night that Rían went after Chloe, Petra had been on the phone. She'd been talking to *Hugh*—I know it. She said we had to stay together, that the Ciorcal Iomlán had begun." I wriggled out of

Adam's embrace, grabbed the papers stacked on the table, and found the ones with the swirls and writing. "What did you say 'Iomlán' meant, Adam?"

He looked over my shoulder. "I'm not sure. I think it means f—"

Chloe interrupted. "It means the full circle."

I swung around to her. "How do you know that?"

"It's part of our Knights' oath, from the original Irish translation. 'Nourished by earth, warmed by fire, quenched by water, and enabled by air, bound are we until the circle comes full.' An Ciorcal Iomlán."

The pounding in my head slowed and released me from its painful clutches. "What is all this about?" I whispered.

Chloe glanced at Sebastian nervously.

"Caitlin!" I jumped back, banging into Adam. "Oh my god! I completely lost it in front of her."

"It's okay," Adam reassured me. "Áine got her out of the room before the worst of it."

"I have to talk to her."

Adam wrapped his arms tighter around me. "We need to figure out what we're going to do about Petra."

"No. I need to talk to Caitlin first." I shook off his arms and ran to find my best friend. I peeked into the sitting room. Matthew was there, glued to the TV. No Caitlin.

I went up to Áine's room. Inside, Caitlin stood at the window. I followed her gaze over the lush farmland that spread in a green haze into the horizon. She drummed her nails impatiently on the windowpane and swung around as soon as my boots clattered on the floorboards of the room.

"I'm going to leave you girls to chat." Áine jumped off the bed. She threw me a warning look before she closed the door.

"What was all that about?" Caitlin half laughed with a wild look in her eyes. "I mean, seriously, weird phone calls, Rían molesting me, you freaking out at Chloe, and all that friggin wind and slamming doors! It was like a scene from *The Exorcist* or something. Then Áine abducts me and keeps me in here against my will for half an hour." She winced and rubbed her temples. "And now I've got a god-awful headache. What on earth is going on?"

Áine! "Caitlin, I'm so sorry. This is . . . complicated."

"What I saw downstairs was a lot more than 'complicated.' What are you hiding from me?"

"I . . . I can't tell you."

Caitlin flinched like she'd been stung. Her wide eyes suddenly narrowed, and her mouth settled into a tight line. "I see."

"No, you don't. Caitlin, there's stuff going on here that you wouldn't understand."

"Try me." For a second, her eyes opened again, honest and accepting. The urge to tell her everything was almost unbearable. Then a knock sounded on the door.

"Mind if I come in?" Adam asked, popping his head around the door.

"Sure," I said. Part of me was relieved he'd stopped me from spilling the beans, but it would have been so nice not to have to lie to her anymore.

"I'm sorry about earlier," Adam said. "We'd just discovered that Petra might be cheating on Megan's dad."

"Cheating?" Caitlin raised an eyebrow and looked uncertainly at me.

I sighed. "I didn't want to tell." I avoided her eyes as the lies sent prickling heat to my cheeks.

"That wasn't what I was expecting." She moved away from the window and crossed her arms. The gesture mirrored the barrier I saw going up in her eyes.

Adam's mouth curled into a lopsided smile. "What were you expecting?"

"I don't know . . . something major, like Chloe and Megan in a showdown over Rían . . ." She looked up at Adam nervously.

Adam's eyes went dark. "No. We're all good."

"Oh shite, I should learn to keep my trap shut. I didn't mean to—"

"Honestly, it's okay, Caitlin. Now, Matthew is banging on about not getting crisps and Coke."

"Okay. I guess I'll go down and . . . hang on a second." She paused at the door and then swung around. "If this is just about Petra, then why did you make

Áine take me out of the room? And what was that stuff about Knights?" She looked back and forth between us. "You're lying to me."

I took a deep breath, preparing myself to be honest when Adam stepped forward.

"I'm sorry. We're all sorry, but we need to lie to protect ourselves and you." I stopped breathing. What was he doing? Caitlin watched openmouthed, saying nothing. "We can't tell you the truth, and if you ask us questions, we'll have to lie. So it's best if you don't ask."

Caitlin swallowed hard. "This is about more than gangs and girlfriends, isn't it?"

Adam slowly nodded.

"And Chloe's not just a regular schoolgirl, is she?"

Adam shook his head.

"Are you in on this, Megan?"

I hoped Adam knew what he was doing. "Yes."

She walked back to me and put her face right up to mine. "I'm your best friend. Why won't you tell me the truth?"

From the corner of my eye, I could see Adam shaking his head. "I can't. You'll just have to trust me."

"Trust you? Why should I, when you don't trust me?" Her face twisted into one I didn't recognize. "I've kept the DeRíses' secrets, I've covered for you, lied for you, and yet you still shut me out!" A strangled sob escaped her throat. "Well, I'm done," she said, sliding her eyes from mine to Adam's. "Done!" She stormed from the room, leaving an aching silence behind.

Adam wrapped his arms around me. "Megan, I—"

"Don't!" I snapped, pushing his arms away. "Don't touch me."

Adam looked like I'd just slapped him. "Megan, this is the way it has to be. This is why we don't have friends."

I stepped back and glared at him. "I am not you!"

"And what's that supposed to mean?"

"It means I haven't grown up in this twisted little cocoon. I want freedom, I want friends, and I want honesty!" My voice caught as I crumpled to the floor, dropping my face into my hands. "I really thought I had something special here. I had Caitlin. My dad had Petra. And now I find out that I've dragged my poor dad into this messed-up world I'm a part of. Do you have any idea how that makes me feel?"

Adam's arms fell to his side.

"And I had you." I blinked at him through a haze of bitter tears. "I . . . I love you, so much that it hurts." I clawed at the front of my sweater like it was an obstacle to my feelings. "I want you—I *need* you—but there's always something in the way."

Adam clasped his hands in front of him. "I don't know what to tell you, Megan. I don't know what you want."

"I want my life back."

"That life ended as soon as you evoked your element."

The urge to scream burned in the back of my throat. "It doesn't have to be this way. Open your eyes and look around, Adam. Your world is changing. The Knights are changing, the Order is changing, even the rules are changing." I threw my arms in the air in exasperation.

He caught my hands midair and looked at me with hauntingly sad eyes. "Do you honestly think that I've never felt exactly how you're feeling now?" The blue in his eyes began to swirl erratically. "I watched my mother and father die; I've been moved from town to town, country to country, outrunning an enemy that wants my family. I've had friends, great friends, but those friendships only brought me guilt and sadness, fear that I'd endangered them. Sometimes it's easier for everyone involved if you don't say hello in the first place. It's safer that way." He loosened the grip on my wrists and lowered my hands. "Let Caitlin go. It's better for her. It was bound to happen sooner or later."

I glared at him, feeling all the strength in me ebb away. "I hate you." I regretted the words before I said them, but at that moment, I did hate him. I hated everything he represented.

His eyes dulled, and his face fell still. "That's just perfect. Maybe you should continue down this imma-ture path of self-pity and follow that elemental pull of yours into Rían's arms. You might find what you're looking for."

The sight of him leaving sliced through my heart. My words echoed in my head, mixing with images of Dad's happy, loving face and Caitlin's look of utter hurt. I barely made it to the bathroom, where I threw up every bit of resentment in my body, over and over again.

Twenty-one

DECISIONS

Adam drove me home in silence. Part of me wanted to hug him tight, but I couldn't get past how he'd handled Caitlin.

When we'd called Fionn, he'd accepted the news calmly and had assured us that Petra wasn't a threat. He and Cú were going to be back in Cork in the morning, and he said they would speak with us then. It suddenly felt like everyone knew what was going on except me.

"I'm not leaving you alone here tonight. I'll sleep in the car. I'll be just down the road," Adam said as he pulled up outside my house.

I leaned against the headrest, swallowing back the tears. "I don't hate you."

"I know." He gripped the steering wheel and gazed out the windshield. "Maybe you're right. Maybe it is time to burst the twisted bubble we live in."

"Adam, I—"

"I'll see you in the morning." The tone of his voice made it clear he was done talking. I stepped from the car, and he drove away with his eyes fixed ahead of him.

I let myself into the house, feeling like a hollowed-out version of myself. Dad and Petra were deep in conversation over a glass of wine. Dad laughed at something Petra said, and she smiled back with eyes that reflected his laughter. They looked so happy, but it was lies. All lies.

"Megan!" Dad said, seeing me standing at the door. "Come in and join us."

"Thanks, Dad, but I'm going to go catch up on some reading. Do you mind?"

Petra turned to face me. "We haven't had a chance to talk yet, Megan."

I glanced at her. "Oh, yes. There's so much we have to discuss, isn't there, Petra?"

Her eyes froze as she put her glass down. She pressed her lips into a thin line. "Actually, I got a strange call today. I was sure I heard your name, but we seemed to get cut off. Did you need me for something?"

My heart thudded erratically. "You must have heard wrong. I don't even have your number."

She forced a smile. "Funny that."

"Anyway, good night, Dad."

"Sleep well, Meg."

That night, I fell into an uneasy sleep. I was plagued by images of Caitlin's face as our friendship fell apart, and the sound of me saying "I hate you" to Adam over and over. After waking up with a racing heart for the third time, I lay on my bed and watched as the black dark of night softened with the first hint of a new day. I wished the time away, thinking of Adam in his car down the road. I was just about to go outside to him when a text came in.

In the morning, let's go tell Caitlin the truth. You deserve a best friend. We all do.

I could hardly believe my eyes. It took me all of two seconds to make up my mind. I crawled out of bed, threw on my clothes from earlier, tiptoed down the stairs, and quickly slipped out the door. As soon as I was clear of the house, I picked up my pace, running until I got to Adam's car. The early sun had just peeked over the horizon, and the air still clung to the rich, earthy smells of the night.

Adam's door opened as I approached. He emerged, deep violet shadows carved under his bloodshot eyes. "I'm so sorry," he said.

I pulled up short, stopping myself from running into his arms. "What I said earlier was . . . horrible."

"No, it was exactly what I needed to hear. You were right. This vicious Order cycle can only continue as long as the Marked allow it. We can change that, starting with Caitlin." He looked at me from under his thick lashes.

"You're right too. I don't understand what it's like to be you, and I can't imagine what it was like growing up with the constant fear of being discovered."

He shoved his hands deep into his jacket pockets and rocked on his heels. "Yeah, but what's worse? Hiding who we are from the people we trust, or the people we don't trust finding out where we're hiding? Maybe it would be easier if we let people in."

I closed the gap between us and mirrored his stance, tucking my hands into my own pockets to stop them from reaching for him. "We don't have to tell her. I wasn't giving you an ultimatum. I was just angry."

He drew closer and leaned his forehead to mine, resting it there. "It's about time we started walking our own path. Why follow the one that has failed so many others? We're telling Caitlin."

I sighed as I felt the relief flood my hollow insides. "Thank you."

He placed a hand on my hip. "You should go home and get some sleep. It's going to be a long day."

I closed my eyes and leaned into him. "I can't sleep." Tears threatened again. "I won't be able to relax until I've set things right."

Adam glided his hand to my lower back and pulled me close. "You know what always makes me feel better? The water."

"We can't just head off in the middle of the night."

"It's morning . . . just about. Come on," he whispered hoarsely, burying his face in my neck before opening the door to his car.

Adam parked outside the yacht club, unlocked the staff entrance, and disappeared inside. A few minutes later, he was running back to the car with a bag and a big grin on his face.

"This is crazy," I said.

"No, this is walking our own path."

Adam untied the yacht from the marina, and we set off. The engine rumbled as we made for open water. I couldn't help smiling at how ironic it was that I had spent my life being scared of water, and now here I was in love with the embodied element of my fear. I chuckled as I thought of my first sailing lesson with Adam and the idiot I'd made of myself.

Under the power of the morning breeze, we glided across the glistening sea in silence. The water had a silken quality under the subtle dawn light. A lone seagull flew beside us, its wings skimming the water as it rode the brisk sea breeze. I watched as Adam worked. He'd changed a little over the past seven months. His tall, sinewy body had broadened and his face had filled out, jaw and cheekbones becoming more prominent. He saw me checking him out and winked, flashing a cheeky grin. I caught my breath, never wanting him more than at that moment.

"Megan," Adam called, breaking my reverie. "Will you drop the sail there for me?"

"Sure."

We were tucked away in a beautiful cove just outside the harbor, hidden by a small island off the shore. The water was sheltered from the winds that gusted up the south coast, and the boat danced with the light lapping of softly rolling waves. The sky gave way to a hazy blue, with only a few wispy clouds floating high above.

It felt good to be here with him, away from all the problems that awaited us when we returned. "You were right. I feel better already," I breathed as I turned to him. He folded his arms around me and gave me the softest of kisses. The energy built between us, merging and swirling above our heads, until my hair rose up and flicked around. Adam pulled away, keeping his eyes closed. He was still holding my face when his breath caught.

"Are you all right?" I asked him.

"Shush," he whispered, nodding. "I'm fine, just hang on a second."

I put my hands up to his face, feeling the stubble that had become thicker and darker over time. His breathing settled and his eyes opened. "If I promise never to be a dick again, will you promise not to hate me?"

"Adam, I was angry, my element was all over the place, my best friend had just—"

"Megan, for a second, you truly hated me—I felt it in your element."

"No, I didn't. You know that sometimes the elements act independently, like with Rían and wh—"

He put his thumb over my lips and caressed them into silence. "It's okay. Just promise me you won't hate me."

"Adam, I will never hate you. I love you."

"Good, because . . . I'm not saying no anymore. I'm ready when you're ready."

"Are you saying what I think you are?"

"Yes. I'm not letting the Order dictate my life for even another minute. You're the most important thing to me in the world. I want you, all of you, forever."

I leaned in and brushed my lips against his. "I'm ready," I murmured between kisses.

I heard his breath catch as he pulled me closer, molding his body against mine. "Now?"

"Now, tomorrow, next week, I don't mind. I'm ready when you are."

He swallowed hard. "Let's just see how it goes, okay?" He put his head down on my shoulder. "I'm nervous."

"So am I."

He sighed. "I love you. And again, I promise to never be a dick."

"Don't make promises you can't keep."

"Hey!" He grabbed me by the waist and squeezed until I was laughing uncontrollably.

A thousand butterflies had taken up residence in my stomach. "Let's go for a swim."

"Really?" he said eagerly, already pulling off his sweater.

I eyed him and gave him a wicked smile. "Oh, I'd say anything to get you to strip." Adam froze with his head half out of his top. He narrowed his eyes. I pulled off my shirt, and his jaw dropped. "I'm joking. Now stop staring at me—you're making me feel self-conscious."

Adam blushed and spun around, getting one foot stuck in his jeans as he tried to step out of them. He lost his balance and caught himself on the railing.

"Will you warm it up a few degrees for me?" I asked, trying to sound more sure of myself than I felt. I took off the rest of my clothes and wrapped a blanket around me, forcing my eyes shut for a second and searching for the confidence I knew was inside me . . . somewhere. This was Adam, after all.

He laughed. "Done. We have our own little piece of the tropics in there." He ran his eyes over me, and my heart hammered in my chest. "Is this part of your whole seduction technique?"

"What, me wrapped in a tartan picnic blanket? It's pretty sexy, isn't it?"

"You've never looked more gorgeous." He took me

in his arms, our skin hot on each other's bodies. Then, without warning, Adam jumped off the yacht with me in his arms. He was kissing me so hard, I couldn't even scream, let alone draw a breath. We sank below the undulating waves, leaving my blanket floating on the surface. Before I had time to panic, I realized I could breathe. We were in a pocket of air.

Adam kissed me again with such passion, it nearly stopped my heart. Under the water, I could see our powers, caressing us as they swirled and sparkled like golden sunlight. Adam pulled me closer, and I wrapped myself around him, forgetting my self-consciousness. We floated on a cushion of water, the color of our skin transformed by the magical, molten glow of our elements, and the hazy blue light that filtered from the sky above. Adam held out his hand and nodded to the surface. I nodded back, reached over, and took his hand. He pulled us from the shadow of the underside of the yacht and up toward the bright water.

This was it. I was finally getting Adam, all of him. My head broke the surface, and he pulled me aboard into his strong, warm arms. My heart jumped wildly in my chest.

"Are you absolutely sure?" he whispered breathlessly, searching my eyes.

"One hundred percent. I've never wanted or needed anything more in my life." I stood on my tiptoes and pulled him to me, our minds and bodies totally immersed in each other.

I woke up with the weight of Adam's arm draped over me. He was still fast asleep, his chest slowly rising and falling. I snuggled into his side and allowed myself to relive what had just happened, but came up blank. The last thing I remembered was kissing after we got out of the water. I put my arm over Adam's chest and shivered. How long had we been asleep? I pushed myself up, wrapped the blanket around me, and nudged Adam. He still slept soundly.

Trying to clear the confused fog from my mind, I got up and padded over to where I'd discarded my clothes earlier. I pulled on my jeans and sweater, then sat down beside Adam again. I shook his arm and whispered in his ear, "Time to wake up, Adam." His skin felt oddly cool. "Adam, wake up!" He still didn't budge.

A rush of fear ran through me. "Adam?" I put my hands on either side of his face and shook him again. His arm that was draped across his chest fell to the side, completely limp. I stared at it in horror. Blood pumped through me, swishing by my ears. "Adam!" I shouted, tapping his cheek. "Open your eyes! Please?"

But there was nothing.

Twenty-two

CLUAÍN

My hair whipped against my face. I felt as if someone was gripping my throat, slowly squeezing
until it hurt to breathe. What had happened? What had
I done? Why couldn't I remember? Wind lashed around
the boat, rocking it viciously. I lifted one of Adam's eyelids and gasped. There was no trace of green, and his
usual blue elemental swirl was gone, changed to a dead-
flat black. Not daring to breathe, I checked the other
one. It was the same.

"Adam!" I screamed, feeling my emotions escape from
the confines of my control. My element was bubbling
and fizzing inside my whole body. It felt unfamiliar,
burning through my veins, working its way to my heart

and gripping it tight. My head was fuzzy, everything was wrong . . . so wrong.

"Adam!" I screamed again. I froze as I caught my reflection in his eye. Horrified, I leaned closer. My eyes were gleaming white, shimmering like crystals. I rubbed them, expecting them to feel different—hot, maybe— but my fingers were numb, my senses dulled. Then the torrential rain started. It fell in great gray sheets, slicing down around us. The waves came crashing in like walls, smashing against our yacht.

I felt nothing but the burning ache in my chest, and the scream trapped deep within me, bursting to come out. I turned my face away from Adam's motionless body and looked at the clouds that billowed above our heads. Completely disconnected from everything other than pain and Adam, I picked him up in my arms, surprised at how light he felt. The wind closed in on us, lifting us high in an icy-cold cocoon of cloud and air.

Then it was quiet. Too quiet. Panic exploded through me as I realized Adam was no longer in my arms. I grasped at the foggy haze around me, searching for the substance of his body in the misty nothingness. "Adam!" I gasped, feeling like I was going to burst with the emotion.

"Don't worry, you're still holding him tight."

I whipped my head around, trying to find the source of the voice. "I don't have him. I can't see him!"

"He's right here." A warm sensation filled my heart

like a temporary connection to my human emotions. The tears started spilling down my face.

"What's going on? What have I done?" Whispers filled my ears and then began to materialize, swirling in the mist, grainy hues of beige gathering form. The haze darkened and moved toward me. It was the Sidhe—my spirit guide. I hadn't seen him since before I evoked my element. "You!" I gasped. He smiled, his face more ghostly than I remembered. His long beard and white hair faded into the wispy clouds that weaved between us. "What happened to Adam? What's happening to me?"

His words floated through the air, but his lips didn't move. "Adam is still in your arms. You can't feel him because you can't feel yourself."

I looked down and ran a hand down each arm. He was right. I felt nothing. "But I feel my tears," I said, putting my hands up to my face, to the water still pouring from my eyes.

The Sidhe crouched down beside me, took both my hands, and held them in his. "You still have the connection to the elements, just not your body."

I shook my head in confusion, staring at his unspeaking lips while trying to focus on his words. "I don't understand."

"What do you feel in here?" He placed his hand over my heart, and I flinched.

"It stings."

"What else?"

"I don't know," I cried, shaking my head. I felt a twinge deep in my chest.

"What else?" the Sidhe repeated.

I focused on this new sensation. It was warm, nearly hot. I felt its grip on my heart, like it was hugging it tight, making it difficult to breathe. I forced in a deep breath and allowed this new sensation to flow through me, letting it ripple to my fingers and toes. The Sidhe smiled. I tore my eyes from him to my chest. "Adam," I whispered.

"Yes," the Sidhe said, removing his hand. The water that had been pouring from my eyes pooled onto the gray haze by my knees. My hand ached to skim its glistening, reflective surface. "Give in to it," the Sidhe urged.

I let my hand glide to the sparkling puddle and watched as the liquid followed my hand like mercury on a smooth surface. I gasped. "How can I do that?" I whispered. "Adam is the water element."

"Look," the Sidhe said, pointing back to the pool.

On my hands and knees, I bent over the liquid and gazed deep into its glazed surface.

I saw my crystal-white eyes, but there, right at the center . . . blue. A blue so unusual I recognized it immediately. It was Adam's blue. His element. I fell away from the water as the realization hit. I'd taken Adam's element!

"NO!" I shouted, pushing myself farther away from

223

the reflection I didn't want to see. "I couldn't have done this. NO! NO! NO!" I grasped my hand over my heart and reached out to the warm feeling that hugged it, knowing it was true. The tears started to pour again, like little waterfalls I knew weren't real tears. "How did this happen? How do I give it back?"

"It is nearly time for An Ciorcal Iomlán. This is what you're supposed to do, but it's too early."

"The full circle! What is it?"

"It is what you were selected for."

"The alignment?"

He shook his head. "It is too late for that."

"No, it's not. We're ready for the solstice."

"You must prepare for the Filleadh ar an Bandia."

"I don't know what that is," I protested.

"You are the Cluaín. The answer you seek is in the stone."

"What stone? Why won't you just tell me?"

"The Cluaín cannot be guided. You already have the answers you seek." A ghost of a smile made his lips twitch, and his form began to swirl again. "I leave you in good hands."

"Whose hands?"

"Those who surround you with protection and who seek the true end."

The Sidhe started to fade. "Don't go!" I grasped at his brown cloak, but it disintegrated in my fingers, swirling away to join the rest of the clouds that had begun spinning around me. The burning pain returned. Now I knew it was the sting of Adam's element fighting for space with my own. I felt the solidness of Adam's body in my arms again. The relief of being able to feel him was quickly replaced by fear. The cushioning cloud that had been carrying us dissipated, leaving me sitting on the wet grass outside of the DeRíses' house. I cradled Adam on my lap while the air whipped and the rain fell. I screamed out, not the powerful roar of an angry element but the cry of a girl with a broken heart. I put my hands on either side of his face, and willed with every ounce of my being to put his element back in him. Nothing happened. It was wrapped too tightly around my heart. I tried again, holding my breath, all the energy I had, until it left me breathless and exhausted.

The outside lights flickered on, and I heard a door slam.

"Megan?" Fionn called from the front door. He ran toward us, followed quickly by Rían, Áine, and Chloe. Rían landed down beside me with a thud. "Megan, what happened?" I looked back at him, unable to speak. "Holy shit! What's wrong with your eyes?"

Chloe knelt beside us and put a hand on either side of my face. "Megan, you have to tell us what happened." The sting of tears built behind my nose, causing my head to ache. I couldn't cry. It was like the tears were frozen, trapped inside me. The rain continued to pour down; it lashed at my face with such brutality that it stung. I welcomed the pain.

"We have to get them inside," Fionn ordered. "Now!"

"Finally, you're awake," Adam said. "I thought I'd lost you for a while there."

I tried to sit up, but my head was fuzzy and dizzy.

"Take it easy," he said.

"How long have I been asleep?"

"About two hours." He traced his finger over my shoulder, down my arm, and along my waist and hip. "That was quite something, wasn't it?"

I risked moving again and pulled myself closer, molding my body against his. "Hang on a second." I looked at him, confused, and then my stomach twisted and churned as reality gripped me. "This isn't real, is it?"

Adam smiled and wrapped me in the blanket. "It's real here." He put his hand over my heart.

"I don't want to wake up."

"You have to. We need you."

"Stay with me!"

"I'll be here." The heat built in my heart until it burned, and the bitter sting of consciousness engulfed me.

Twenty-three

CONSEQUENCES

Four worried faces peered at me as I lay on Adam's bed. My arm ached. I glanced down to see the source of the pain, but it was my own hand clenching Adam's.

He was still unconscious, his chest rising and falling with clockwork precision. I sat up and ran my other hand down his cheek. He didn't react, but my face tingled. Curious, I touched him again. Yes, I definitely felt my caress on Adam's face, like it was my own. Shock rippled through me at the strange sensation. I looked down at my hand connected with his and felt my grip back. I smiled sadly and pried my fingers away, allowing my tears to fall onto our hands, sensing as the wetness hit his hand through mine.

"Megan." Fionn's voice sounded far away. "Megan!" he repeated. I snapped out of my stupor and slowly turned to face him. "Megan, we need you to tell us what happened." I didn't know where to start. I felt my gaze being drawn to Adam, but Fionn grabbed my chin and pulled it back in his direction. "Megan, stay focused! Talk to us."

"Let me try." Áine removed Fionn's hand from my chin and sat down beside me. "Megan, we need to help you and Adam, but you have to tell us what happened." She leaned over and picked up his hand. I gasped, feeling as if she were holding mine, sensing her element fizz under his skin.

I stared up at Áine, wanting to speak, but couldn't find my voice. She gazed into my eyes and winced. I opened my mouth, trying again, and finally found the connection to my tongue. "He's here," I whispered, putting one hand to my heart and the other to my head.

Áine cocked her head and peered at me closer. "He's here," she explained, putting her arm on Adam's chest.

"No." I took her hand and put it over my heart. "He's here."

Áine glanced from me to Fionn, shaking her head.

"She's still delirious," Rían said. He paced up and down the room, his strides long and impatient. "Shouldn't we smack her or something? We don't have time for this."

Fionn turned to me again. "Megan, what do you mean?"

I focused on Fionn, willing him to see what I felt, Adam's element pulsing back at him. Fionn stared at me, searching deep in the glittering crystal white of my eyes. Then he pulled back sharply.

"It can't be!" Fionn paled and glanced from Adam to me in shock. "No!"

"What?" Rían came up and stared into my face. "What is it?"

"Adam . . . Adam's element . . ." Fionn said.

Áine ran to the other side of the bed and raised Adam's eyelids, revealing black lifeless eyes. A small cry escaped her lips. "You took his element! How?"

"I don't know," I spluttered. "I woke up and he was unconscious, and then the storm took over and we were floating and, and . . ." I broke off. How could I even begin to explain what had happened? "The Sidhe said I was the Cluaín, that this was what I was selected for . . . but he said it was too early." I shook my head in confusion. "He said something else, some more Irish . . . I didn't understand."

"The Sidhe visited you?" Fionn avoided my eyes.

"Yes, he said . . ." I racked my brain, trying to remember the strange, ethereal conversation. "He said the answer was in the stone."

"Christ, could he not have told you what it was?"

229

"I asked him, but he said I already had it."

Fionn paced the room, rubbing the back of his head incessantly. "So it's true. I need to speak to Hugh."

Rían's eyes narrowed. "What's true?"

Fionn winced. "Don't worry about it now." His eyes flicked between Adam and me with a mixture of horror and panic etched into face. I reached for Áine. I didn't want her forgiveness for this, but I wanted to explain. "Áine, I—"

"Wait," she said abruptly. "Guys, would you mind giving Megan and me a minute alone?"

"Now is hardly the time for girly chats!" Rían spat.

"Just give me five minutes."

Fionn walked over to the other side of the bed and ran his hand over Adam's face before resting it on his shoulder. "How could I have let this happen?"

"Fionn, stop blaming yourself," Áine said. "Please, let me speak with Megan. We'll sort this out."

"I should have put a stop to this earlier."

Áine's voice softened. "You know Adam never would have listened."

With a sigh, Fionn tapped Adam's shoulder and reluctantly left the room with Rían in his wake.

Áine turned her attention to me. "Now, tell me what happened, from the beginning." All traces of anger were gone. Her voice was full of genuine concern.

I stroked Adam's cheek, reveling in the strange sensation

of my own touch. "We . . ." I gulped back a sob. "Oh, Áine, I thought I had it under control. I was sure we were ready for the next step! Adam was reluctant, but I convinced him that it would be okay." I began to shake as I relived the events.

"You slept together."

"I don't remember." Heat crept up my neck and across my head, leaving me with goose bumps. "We were kind of working toward it, then . . ."

"What? Go on."

"That's the thing. I don't know. I only remember waking up. After a little while, I realized that Adam was more than just asleep, and I started to freak out. Then I saw my eyes." I raised my fingers and traced the outline of them. "They'd changed, and I felt . . . his power, in me."

I dragged my eyes from Adam's peaceful face over to Áine's troubled one. "The storm picked up—it was crazy, like a hurricane or something. Was that me?"

Áine nodded. "Most likely. If you have the water element too, I can only imagine the damage that could cause. What I don't understand is how you're controlling all that power."

I looked down at my hands. "Am I dangerous?"

"You should be, but . . . I don't know. Let's worry about that later. What else happened?"

"I don't really know. The Sidhe said all this stuff about

being the Cluaín, that I was chosen for this reason, but I'd taken too early."

"And the answer was in the stone?"

I nodded.

"And the Cluaín is you?"

"That's what he said . . ." My mind raced.

"I've never heard of 'Cluaín' before." Áine looked at me strangely, like she was seeing me for the first time. "Mind if I try something?"

"What?"

"I've always felt a pull to you, we all have, but we just assumed it was because you were the fourth element. What if there was something else, something more powerful?"

"I don't understand."

"You know that zing we get when we touch each other? What if that's more than recognition?"

Slowly it dawned on me what Áine was getting at. I peeked over at Adam again, and my heart skipped a beat, then thudded erratically.

"Let me try." She held out her hand.

"No!" I pulled away and sat on my hands. "I've done enough damage."

"Megan, we need to know what we're dealing with. Now take my hand."

I stared at her for what seemed like an eternity and then glanced back at Adam. My heart was racing so fast, I was sure it would explode. "Get away from me!"

I jumped up and stumbled toward the door, but my legs collapsed as I blacked out.

"Back already?" Adam's face smiled into mine through a fog of confusion.

"Adam." I tried to hug him but felt no substance. "What's happening?"

"You know what's happening."

I shook my head. "I have to figure this out."

"You heard the Sidhe; the answer is in the stone." Adam's presence wavered.

"Don't leave!"

"I'm not leaving. I'm here until you figure this out. It's quite comfortable." He smirked, but there was sadness in his eyes. "I'm tired." He started to fade again.

"Adam, please! Stay!"

His image melted away, and faint laughter echoed in the distance.

"Ticktock, ticktock," a girly voice whispered. The laughter came again and then trailed off, making me doubt if I'd ever even heard it. But it came again, louder this time.

"Ticktock, it's nearly time."

I whirled around, trying to locate the source, when a ghostly image appeared like a void in the haze. Suddenly I was falling toward it at terrifying speed. I couldn't stop. I went right through, and like a bubble popping, it was gone, leaving residue on my skin.

"It's mine," the voice whispered, and faded away.

When I woke, I was home in my own bed. Dad sat beside me, a worried look on his face. "Megan, you're making a habit of this."

"Oh, Dad." I started sobbing and climbed into his arms, something I hadn't done since I was a little girl.

"Hey, hey, what's wrong? Did the storm give you that much of a fright? Don't worry, it's all over now." He hugged me tight. "I guess your instincts around the water were right. I will never let you set foot in a boat again."

"Um . . . what?" I asked, wondering what story he'd been spun.

"The club yacht. The hurricane." He pulled away and inspected me more closely. "Are you sure you're okay? I can call the doctor."

"No, don't. I'm fine. It was just all such a shock."

"Thank goodness Adam got you back to the marina before the worst of it hit. I can't bear to imagine what would have happened if he hadn't. What on earth were you doing out there so early, anyway? Don't ever go off like that without telling me! Petra and I were at our wits' end."

I felt the blood drain from my face. "Adam—" I gasped.

"Is fine. Stop worrying. Fionn said he's just a bit worn-out from his adventure, like you. He said you were so exhausted when you got back to their house that you fell asleep on the couch. He thought you'd be more comfortable here." I nodded, not sure how long I'd been home or how Adam was. Did I still have his element in my eyes? My eyes! I squeezed them shut and jumped up, running for the bathroom. "Megan, are you okay?" Dad shouted after me.

I slammed the door behind me and anxiously looked into the mirror. They were my normal sludgy green. I sighed with relief. "I'm fine—I'll be out in a sec."

"I'll make some breakfast. Come down when you're ready." I went to splash water on my face, and with only the slightest movement, water floated up from the sink like a bubble. I lowered my head to the floating liquid and allowed my face to break the tension of the water. It splashed back into the sink. I held out a hand and flicked a towel over to me. My element was unaffected, and I still seemed to have control of the water. But Áine had never answered me—was I dangerous?

As soon as I got downstairs, Dad handed me a mug of tea. "Hot and sweet, just the way you like it."

"Thanks, Dad."

"Can you believe all this?" Dad gestured to the TV, which was on mute.

I stared at the screen, taking in the horrifying pictures of wrecked businesses, trashed beaches, and dead fish washed up with debris all through the town. "Oh my god."

"It's crazy, isn't it? Half the marina has been wiped out, and we have several trawlers and yachts still unaccounted for. The town is a complete mess."

"This can't be happening." Blood drained from my face, and the room spun around me. I wobbled to a chair and sat down hard. I could not have caused this. Could I? I brought my knees up to my chest and rocked myself back and forth, trying to ease the panic that flooded through me. Dad's voice slowly brought me back to the present.

"Megan, it's okay. It's all over now. Listen, are you going to be all right here today? I have to get down to the marina to help clean things up."

I nodded, not taking my eyes off the TV.

"Are you sure?" he asked worriedly. "I'll stay if you need me."

My eyes shot up to his. "NO! Oh . . . sorry, Dad, it's just so terrible. Of course I'll be fine. I'll get dressed and go downtown and see if I can do anything to help."

"I'd prefer you stay out of town, Meg. Why don't you take it easy here for the day instead?"

I shrugged noncommittally.

As soon as Dad left, I got dressed and headed into town to survey the damage for myself. I couldn't believe my eyes. Half the marina was underwater. Yachts with broken masts were stacked up on top of each other, while others lay on their sides, smashed to pieces. Cars had been washed off the pier and were floating in the water. Two men darted past me and headed down the steep stone steps toward the water. Voices drifted up from below, and I froze. In the shallow water, a whale had been beached. Dozens of people stood fully clothed, trying to help it. This was my fault, all of it. In that moment, I hated my element. I wanted it out of me, to be rid of the thing that had ruined my life. But then I realized: If the elements had caused this destruction, they could fix it too. I felt my eyes change as the wind began to whip my hair upward, and my feet lost connection with the road. I focused on the whale, slowly moving him into the water while an astonished crowd looked on.

"There must be some sort of undertow or something!" one woman shouted as she and all the others kept pouring buckets of water over the whale. "Look at the water! Holy Mary mother of God, everyone, get onto the pier!"

The water rose up like a tsunami and started rushing toward the shore. I opened my eyes, making sure everyone was on the pier, and then let the water drop. The shocked onlookers stood back, watching as the whale was picked up by the tide and drawn out into deeper waters. As soon as the whale hit the depths, he disappeared below the surface.

One wrong righted. On to the next. I scanned the scene and noticed a car toppled over another one. I flicked a hand to pick up the wind, and a vortex started swirling. I guided it across the street, dragging the car. People were scared now, running for cover, their faces wide-eyed in confusion. They probably thought another hurricane or tornado was hitting. A woman stopped suddenly, pointed at me, and called to the others, but I didn't care. I watched as my vortex worked its way up the road, clearing the way.

"MEGAN! What the hell are you doing?" a voice said loudly. "Stop it, NOW!" I spun around to find Áine glaring at me. I hardly recognized her with her scowling face. She grabbed me by the sleeve and dragged me away from the crowd, who was now staring at me. "What are you trying to do? Get us all outed? Jesus Christ!"

"How did you find me?"

"How do you think, you plonker? I've been doing my bit in fixing up this mess—a little more subtly, I might add, than I see you doing . . . this. And you shouldn't be using Adam's element!"

"Adam! How is he?"

Her face softened, and the corners of her eyes turned down. "No change."

"Can we go see him?"

"Fionn said we had to keep you away from the house while he figured out what to do."

My heart sank as rejection washed over me. "Please, Áine. I need to see him."

Áine looked around at the chaos and sighed. "Okay, I'll sneak you in, but first I've got to fix this." She glared at all the people who were staring at us, openmouthed. Her eyes flicked to almost entirely ebony, just the thinnest of acid green flashing around her giant pupil. I stepped away from her as I felt her suggestion seep into my skull. It was like an invasion, unwanted thoughts telling me to unsee the last five minutes, alien memories, forcing their way in until they felt like my own. I pushed them away, rejecting her suggestions, unlike everyone else who was now caught under her spell.

Her eyes flickered between black and green before returning to normal. "Come on, let's get out of here while we can."

We left the group of confused and slightly agitated people at the water's edge and went to get Adam's car, which Áine had parked up the road.

"Your new power seems to be getting very strong," I said, getting in.

She shrugged and started the engine. "I've been practicing. It's easy, really."

"It doesn't feel right to be manipulating people's thoughts, Áine."

She sat bolt upright in the driver's seat and pulled out in the direction of home. "At least I'm not creating hurricanes, burning down houses, and causing general mayhem and destruction."

"Point taken."

"I knew straightaway," she said, relaxing a little as we left the town. "I knew what you'd done."

"What do you mean?"

"With Adam."

"Oh, Áine." I dropped my face into my hands. "It's all my fault."

"No, it's not. It's the element's fault." She glanced at me. "I sense him in you, you know."

"I sense him too. He talks to me." I blushed a little. "When I sleep. I have to figure out how to give him back."

"If you let me into your head, I might be able to speak with him."

I rubbed my brow. "No. I don't think he's here. It's more like he's around me, and in my heart." I paused for a second. "I've been hearing another voice too."

Áine gasped. "Whose?"

"I don't know. She whispers at me and laughs. She keeps saying 'ticktock.' It's really scary."

"You should let me into your head. I might be able to help."

"But you can't read my mind. How could that be of any benefit?"

She pulled in at the DeRíses' and turned to me. "I may not be able to hear what's going on in your brain, but maybe I'll pick up on the other things going on, like Adam, and that other voice."

"Let me think about it, okay?"

"Sure." She put her hand over mine and bit her bottom lip. "There's something else I need to tell you."

Twenty-four

ACCUSATIONS

"Look at this." Áine pulled back her hair and revealed her Mark, showing me the four interlocking circles that made up the symbol of the four elements.

"Yeah?" I said. "What exactly am I supposed to be looking at?"

"Look at the center."

I peered closer at her Mark. There, in the middle of the interlocking circles, was the beginning of another arc.

"No!" I grasped the rearview mirror and turned it down to look at my own Mark. It was identical. "What can this mean?"

"I haven't a clue. But I've a feeling it's something bad," Áine said, getting out of the car.

We went into the house and headed straight up to Adam's room.

Rían was sitting at Adam's side. "Megan, Fionn will freak out if he finds you in here."

"Any change?" I asked, ignoring his comment.

Rían sighed and got up. "Nope."

I sat down beside Adam and ran my hand through his dark hair, brushing it out of his eyes. I traced his eyelids and his strangely cool face, trying to ignore the caress I felt down my own.

"Adam," I whispered.

Rían cleared his throat and mumbled, "Look, I'll give you five minutes, but then I have to let Fionn know you're here. I'm sorry, Meg." He left the room, closing the door quietly behind him.

I fought the tears that stung my eyes, and I gently moved Adam's head to the side to inspect his Mark. The beginning of the fifth arc was stark against his ashen skin.

"I've an idea!" Áine shouted, bursting into the room, bringing with her a draft of cold air and a small brass box.

I sat up. "What do you mean?"

She winced as she opened the box. "The amulet!" She held it out to me. "It glows when it's close to the elements, right? That's how the Knox used it to track the Marked."

"Yes," I said, exasperated. "We know that. What about it?"

"We can use it to track the fifth."

"You think there is one?"

"It would explain the new Mark."

"But I thought the fifth was supposed to be created using all four elements. That doesn't make sense."

"Doesn't it? You've already got two of them, Megan, and I don't know about Rían, but I have a constant urge to give you mine."

I looked from Adam to Áine. "What *is* the fifth element?"

"Supposedly, spirit."

"And you think it's connected to what's happening with me?"

She shrugged. "I don't know, but if there's a link, we might be able to help Adam." She held the amber stone to herself, and its glow intensified. Then as she moved it away, it faded. "Did you see that?"

"Of course I did."

She slowly moved the stone from one side of her body to the other. As the stone passed over her chest, the glowing really illuminated, so much that it was hard to look at. "The source of the element must be in our chests. It's actually kinda freaky."

I looked down at the stone, feeling the strength of its binding as my hand got closer. I carefully moved it to my chest, watching it grow brighter and brighter, then stopped. "You think there's another one of us out there?"

"Maybe."

"Do you think that girl whose voice I heard could be the fifth?"

"The ticktocking one? I have no idea, but you should let me listen."

"I only heard her once."

"Maybe you're just not listening hard enough. Let me in." Her eyes were already flickering black and green. "Only for a minute, okay? If it is the fifth, I might be able to figure out where to start looking for her. Do it for Adam."

I glanced at him. "Okay, but make it quick."

"Clear your mind."

"Wait, don't you need me to put the amulet back in the box?"

"Nah, I've learned to work around it. I'm way beyond that sucker. Now, focus on me." She stared at me with her alien-like eyes and cocked her head to the side. Then it jolted in the other direction. She rushed at me, gripping me by the shoulders, her black, piercing eyes so close to mine that I couldn't concentrate on both. I looked from one to the other, seeing my own horrified expression. I felt weird . . . almost like air was swishing around inside my head. Then her eyes suddenly flickered back to their normal appearance, and she pulled away from me.

I winced at the ache she'd left in my head. "Did you hear anything?"

"Sort of. It was more like a feeling than a sound. They're not voices, but more like . . . audible messages stamped into you."

"What kind of messages?"

"It's the elements—air and water. It's like the previous generations of Marked Ones who had those elements have left a calling card. There're so many."

"But that doesn't help us, Áine." My eyes drifted to Adam as I sifted through the hazy memories of what had happened. "The Sidhe said the answer was in the stone, right?" I moved the amulet over my heart and watched it glow bright and intense. "Maybe we should look for those answers with it." I lifted the heavy chain to put the amulet around my neck.

Áine grabbed my wrist. "Wait! Hugh told us never to wear it."

"Look, we're at a dead end. If I put it on, we might get some answers." Áine's worried eyes glanced between Adam and me, and then she slowly released my wrist. I dropped the chain over my neck. Before I could utter another word, pain ripped through me. I fell back on the bed, frozen by the vicious stabbing in my chest.

"Áine!" I managed to gasp through the searing agony. "What's happening?"

Her frightened eyes washed over me. She leaned

forward and then slumped to the floor, groaning. "I can't get to you. Look! Look at the amulet!"

I rolled onto my side, willing my pain-seized arm to move. The amber glowed brightly, an intense light burning my skin where the pendant rested. I moved the chain and drew a sharp breath. The light wasn't shining from the amulet. It was coming from my skin. The burning sensation eased slightly as I moved the amulet, so I pushed it toward my left shoulder. The white heat burrowed through my body, looking for an outlet, burning everything in its path. I screamed out to Áine.

"Megan, I can't help you!" she cried. "It won't let me near you. I'm going to get someone."

I couldn't get beyond the pain to respond. I stared in horror as a great light burned to the left of my chest, just over my heart. It made its way to the amulet, which radiated the light through its amber, illuminating the room. I couldn't take the pain anymore. I reached over and held Adam's limp hand. The pain felt tight within me, like it had filled the space and had nowhere else to go. Then suddenly it broke free.

I watched as the ribbons of gold slithered from my skin and snaked their way along my arm onto Adam's. They dived into Adam's chest, and his whole body arched upward, only his head and feet remaining on the bed. Then just as quickly as the light had appeared, it disappeared into Adam's body, and he flopped back onto the bed. My pain was gone.

"Megan?"

"Adam?" I mumbled, wiping my eyes and trying to focus on his face. Adam was back. The answer *had* been in the amulet. It had released the water element and returned it to Adam. My pain forgotten, I threw myself in Adam's direction, but fell short as Fionn swooped in and caught me before I made contact.

"Let me go!" I shrieked. I struggled in Fionn's arms, but it was useless. I was still too weakened from what had just happened.

"Get it off her!" Fionn shouted at Rían, who'd followed him in.

Rían removed the amulet and stepped back. "What was that? What did she do?"

"The Marked should NEVER wear the amulet. Don't ever do that again. Rían, put it back in the box."

I struggled against Fionn's grip, and the air whipped up around me, but I reined my power back in and surrendered. I allowed myself to droop in his arms. "The Sidhe was right about the stone. It worked. Adam got his element back," I whispered.

Fionn relaxed his grip and turned me around to face him. "Yes, but you should not have survived that unscathed. You just went through the elemental stripping and kept your power."

"Megan, are you all right?" Adam called, pushing himself up in the bed.

Relief made me dizzy. "I'm fine." I tried to shrug off Fionn's arms, but Fionn tightened his grip again.

"I'm sorry, Megan. But you can't. You can't touch Adam . . . you can't touch any of them."

"What? Why?" I asked, turning my head to Rían, Áine, and Adam. "I would never hurt them."

"You won't, but your element will. Megan, 'Cluaín' means 'deception.' The Cluaín's sole purpose is to remove and combine the elements to enable the release of the fifth."

"You know what's happening to me?" I managed to croak before the sting of tears gripped my throat.

He nodded sadly. "That's what we were coming down to tell you."

"We?" I asked.

"Hugh, Cú, and me."

"You found Hugh?"

"We did. When Hugh suspected what you were, he abandoned the alignment training and started gathering all the information he could. It's what he's been doing since he left here. He's activated An Ciorcal na Fírinne."

"The Circle of Truth," Rían said.

"Yes." Fionn turned his gaze back to me. "Cú, Petra, Hugh—they're all part of it. The things I've learned . . . I've so much to tell you. All of you. Megan, I'm so sorry, but you've already started the cycle of the fifth. I have to find a way to stop it. You can't be near them anymore."

With my world crumbling, I looked in Adam's direction. "You're okay?"

He nodded, his color returning to normal. My eyes dropped to his chest, to the burn the element had left on his skin, and I gasped. The scar was just like one of the swirls from the Cup of Truth and Hugh's notes. I pulled open a few buttons of my blouse and traced my fingers over an identical mark burned into my chest. I couldn't help but realize we'd just witnessed the end of all our hopes and dreams. My heart pulled me to him, and my conscience wrenched me away. Tearing my eyes from his, I walked toward the door.

"No, wait!" Adam called after me, but I didn't dare look back. With each step, my determination grew. I would never allow myself to inflict that kind of pain on him again. A bitter resolve seeped through me, infecting every cell in my body, chilling my heart and binding my emotions in layers of self-hatred. Fionn was right; I could never touch any of them again. I bolted for the door and didn't stop running until I got to the road. I caught my breath and looked back at the DeRíses' house.

It was over.

I wrapped my arms around me and gazed, unseeing, at the road ahead. Randel swooped down and landed on the ground in front of me. I stepped around him. He hopped alongside me, trying to get under my feet.

"Randel, Áine! Leave me alone. I can't . . . I just can't do this right now."

Randel shuffled to the side and dropped his head to his chest. I walked past him and didn't dare look back.

Reminders of the destruction I'd caused littered the ground. Swirling paths of sand and smashed vegetation lined the road where the last of the tidal water had drained from the land. The water in the Bandon estuary, now a murky brown, looked dark and sinister as it raced toward town and the mouth of the harbor. Why hadn't I listened to the warnings? How could I ever have thought I was stronger than the element within me?

A car pulled up next to me. I ignored it for a few minutes, hoping whoever it was would leave me alone. But the car continued to crawl at my pace. I eventually glanced up, ready to tell Chloe, Áine, or whoever it was to go away. But the flash of red in my peripheral vision triggered the breakdown I'd been predicting. Caitlin.

She braked, swung open the door, and got out, closing the gap between us. "Oh, Megan!"

I sank into her arms and cried. We stood in the middle of the road for what seemed like forever.

"I know." She ran her hand down my hair. "I know. Come on, Megan, we've got to get you home." She guided me back to the car, and we climbed in. "Look

at me. I've more snot and tears on me than you have."
She handed me a wad of fast-food napkins. "My place
or yours?"

"I thought you weren't my friend anymore."

"Megan, it would take a lot more than secrets to get
rid of me."

"How did you know where I was?"

"Rían called. He said you needed me right now.
What's going on?"

The secrets and lies pounded in my head, looking for
an escape. "Yours."

"Huh?"

"Let's go to your place. We need to talk."

She raised an eyebrow and nodded. "Talk, talk?"

I nodded.

"My place it is."

Twenty-five

IF TRUTH BE TOLD

Caitlin leaned forward and clutched my knees. "You're taking the piss outta me! I can't believe it."

"I swear it's all true." I held my mug of sweet tea in my hands and tried to absorb the warmth as a chill ran down my spine.

"How could I have not seen any of this?"

I closed my eyes and winced. Hours of crying had left them raw and dry. "We keep it well hidden. Nobody else knows, not even my dad."

"So all the rumors were true! The DeRíses are druids."

"We're not druids!" I tried to open my eyes, but one caught, my lashes stuck together from the tears.

I rubbed it and forced it open. "The Order and the Knights kinda are, though."

"You're a mess," Caitlin said, getting up and opening a cabinet. "Here, try some of these." She threw a bottle of drops at me. "I used half the bottle yesterday. They work a treat, see?" She pointed at her crystal-clear eyes.

"I'm so sorry. I wanted to tell you the truth."

"I can understand why you didn't. My head is still spinning. You're like a magical creature from the dawn of time!"

"No, I'm just a normal girl from the twenty-first century who *inherited* a magical power from the dawn of time."

"Still, it's amazing! What a gift."

"I used to feel that way. Now it seems more like a curse."

She shook her head. "I used to see stuff happening around you, and I'd tell myself I was imagining things. And all that other stuff! Birds, Orders, Knights. It's like I've entered an alternate universe."

"I'm impressed you didn't run screaming from the room."

"Hey, we're only into hour number"—she looked at her watch—"three of this conversation. There's still plenty of time for me to throw a complete fit and get you committed."

"You believe me?"

"How can I not? It explains so much. Don't get me wrong, I think you're delusional, but I still believe you.

Hang on a second . . . that makes me semi-delusional as well, doesn't it?"

"Welcome to my world."

She threw her fist in the air and laughed. "Woo!"

"Caitlin, you have to promise to keep this to yourself. It really is a matter of life and death. Many Marked have died at the hands of the Knox."

"I won't breathe a word, I promise. I feel like the 'cool best friend' in the movies, the girl who gets to know everything. Don't they usually get superpowers too? Maybe I'll become a witch."

I laughed. "Oh, please don't. I don't think I could take much more magic in my life."

"Fine. But if Danu calls on me, I'm answering it!" She crossed her legs, sat in the lotus position, and started chanting while rolling her eyes and fluttering her eyelids.

I thumped her gently. I'd hoped telling Caitlin would make me feel better, but it didn't. Her thrilled acceptance of this magical world just reminded me of my own excitement when I first learned of it, before the elements showed their darker side.

"You do realize that I'm going to wake up in the morning and be one hundred percent convinced that I dreamed this whole conversation?" she said, her eyes still closed.

"I do that every morning. It doesn't get easier to believe with time."

She opened one eye, and her smile dropped. "I'm so sorry about the Adam thing."

My heart lurched. "Me too."

"What are you going to do?"

For a moment, even breathing hurt. "What I have to do. I'm letting him go."

Adam kept calling. I didn't answer. I sat on my bed and watched the phone light up and vibrate until the battery died.

When Dad got home, he slumped against the door. "The harbor's a mess. The clean-up will take longer than I thought. I'm going to shower." He took one look at me and pulled up short. "Everything all right?"

Guilt-stricken, I nodded my head, not meeting his eyes. "Fine. Where's Petra?"

Worry lines crept across his forehead. "I have no idea. There was some damage to her restaurant, so she left early to get the place fixed up, but I haven't heard from her since. She's not answering her cell. I'm getting worried."

Anger at Petra punched me in the stomach, kicking off my emotions again. I despised that he was worrying about her. I gave him a hug. "I'm sure she's fine. She's probably busy cleaning up."

"I hope you're right. It's just unlike her."

"I bet she'll be back before you're out of the shower."

"Megan, you look upset. What's going on?"

I swallowed hard and pushed my emotions back into the pit of my stomach, where they coiled and twisted.

"Adam and I . . . broke up." I somehow managed to keep it together. "It's a long story, but I'm okay."

"I'm not sure I buy that."

"Honestly, Dad, it's been coming for a while. Go, get cleaned up." I forced a smile. "You smell like rotting seaweed."

He hesitated and then wrinkled his nose. "Okay, but we'll talk about this later."

"There's nothing to talk about," I called out to him as he went into his room.

Half an hour later, Fionn showed up at the house. His silhouette was clear through the window by our door. I fled back up the stairs, hoping he didn't see me.

"Megan, couldn't you get that?" Dad asked, stepping over me where I huddled on the top step. He threw on a shirt as he ran down to open the door.

"I can't talk to him. Please, just tell him to go home."

I listened from my perch as Dad and Fionn discussed "the breakup." Fionn was worried, but after enough reassurances from my dad that I was fine, he eventually left.

Dad pushed his damp hair off his forehead and tucked in his shirttails. "I think we need to talk." He put the kettle on. "Do you want some tea?"

I reluctantly nodded and sat down at the table.

Dad joined me. "Fionn seemed genuinely concerned about how you left things with Adam."

"It's complicated, Dad."

"I'm not going to get involved, but if this is really over, be sure to do it right. Loose ends have a habit of blowing in the breeze and getting more tattered and messy with time." He smiled and rubbed my arm. I was a bit taken aback by his uncharacteristically insightful remark. "Don't look so shocked. I was young once, and well . . . it was something your mom used to say."

"Dad, there are so many loose ends, I wouldn't know where to start to fix them up."

Dad set the tea on the table. "I wish I could help, but when it comes to matters of the heart, I'm not so great on the advice front. I'm a good listener, though . . . when you're ready to talk."

I leaned over and gave him a hug. "Thanks, Dad." I wished I was five again and he could make everything better, but I knew that wasn't possible. I needed to get out of the house. I needed to think, and I didn't want to be here when Petra got back. "I think I'll go back to Caitlin's house. Do you mind?"

"Not at all. Maybe you should stay with her tonight, since I'll be at the club late."

I nodded. "Dad, I'm sorry."

"Sorry for what?"

"I'm just sorry, you know, that you have to work so hard fixing up the mess."

"Don't be silly, Meg. These things happen." He laughed. "It should be the storm gods saying sorry, not you."

Caitlin was coming to pick me up, but I needed some air, so I set out to meet her along the way. As I locked the front door, Randel swooped down and landed on my shoulder. "Hey, Randel. You here alone?" Randel squawked and flew across the street, where a figure caught my eye.

Chloe stepped out from the shrubs. "Hey, Meg."

"Chloe." I guess it was inevitable that she would be here. The others wouldn't be allowed to come, and they still thought I needed protection. Couldn't they see that I was the only dangerous person around? "You don't need to be here. You should go back to Rían."

"It's my job, and besides, I thought you might need to talk."

"And what makes you think I'd want to talk to you?" I said, brushing past her.

She fell into step beside me as I headed down the hill. "How are you doing?"

I flashed her a scowl. "How do you think I'm doing?"

I wanted to blame her for everything. She was the one who had wormed her way into our lives. She was the one who flaunted her physical relationship with Rían in my face, making me think I could have one too. With every step I took, my anger grew.

Chloe pulled up in front of me to halt our progress. She nodded at the trees that whipped around with my rage. "You better calm down before you go throwing another hissy fit that will destroy the town even more."

"Don't tell me to calm down! Things are working out nicely for you now, aren't they? You're in with the Knights, and you're buddy-buddy with all the DeRíses. It must feel pretty good to be you at the moment."

Chloe's face turned to stone before she whispered, "You don't know shit."

"Excuse me?"

She threw her arms in the air and screamed at the sky. "You think everything is just la-di-da, don't you?"

I swung back at her. "Oh yeah, everything is just perfect in my life. Look around you, Chloe. This is my life crumbling right before your eyes."

"Megan, there's a lot more going on here than tragic love stories. Don't you see?"

"I don't know what the hell you're talking about."

She moved toward me with her arms outstretched. At first, I thought she was going for my neck. I gasped and tried to duck away, but she grabbed my shoulders and shook me. "This isn't about the Order versus the Knox anymore. This is so much bigger. Forget Adam for one second, and look around you."

I called on the air between us and flung her away from me, landing her hard on her backside. "Stay away from me. My biggest mistake was trusting you. I will never be so naive again."

She sprung to her feet easily. "That's more like it. You need to start using your element defensively. You're going to need it."

My blood ran cold as her words sliced through me. "Tell me what you know."

She shook her head and stepped back. "I've already said too much. I'm bound by the Knights, but . . . I've tried to help you figure it out. Didn't you get the note I slipped you?" She took a deep breath and sighed. "Believe it or not, I actually care about you. I can't stand by and wait for it to happen."

"*You* planted the list of names in my pocket?" My element pulsated, wanting to be unleashed, but I quelled it and focused my attention on Chloe. "Tell me what those names have to do with me."

She clenched her fists. "I can't."

"TELL ME!"

"They . . . they were all Cluaíns. The Order destroyed them. The Circle of Truth has been waiting for the next Cluaín for so long. We've been instructed to protect you at all costs but not to intervene. I just . . . I find it hard to just stand by, to let you deal with this alone."

My element flickered in irritation, blurring my sight and covering my peripheral vision in a haze, like I was peering out a foggy window.

"Deal with WHAT?" Suddenly something hit my face, and I felt like I was lifted right off the ground.

Confused, I lost my balance and fell backward, smacking my back on the concrete. "What th—?" It came again, this time on my other cheek.

"Megan! What's wrong?"

"Chloe!"

"I don't see anything." Chloe grabbed at the air around me. "There's nothing there. What's going on?"

The air whipped around me, looking for my assailant, but there wasn't one. Chloe crouched, with her arms out, waiting for the next attack. I felt groggy, dizzy. My head wobbled on my neck, then hung heavy to the side. I felt the ground moving beneath me, as if I were being dragged. Each bump on my spine stung, like my back was sliding over something hard. My eyes darted around as I tried to make sense of what was happening. I hadn't moved an inch. Black spots obscured my vision, and my ears felt plugged, muffling the sounds around me. A scream, a shout, a thud, and a dull ache rippled through my skull. Then I heard Áine's voice. It was the only clear sound in the cacophony of muted chaos.

"Megan, help us." I pushed past the distressing noises, pain, and dark fog that clouded my brain. Chloe was shouting. Her lips were moving, but I couldn't hear her. I took a deep breath and focused on her mouth, squeezing all other sensations from my mind. Slowly words started to form.

"Megan, what's happening? What's wrong?"

My pulse quickened until the blood raced through my system, flooding me with dread. "It's Áine—she's hurt. She needs my help."

"How do you know?"

"She was in my head. She told me. We have to hurry." I jumped to my feet and started running, not sure where to go next.

Chloe caught up and pulled me to a stop. "Megan, this could be a trap. Stop and think for one minute." She took out her phone. "Let's call the house first."

I didn't want to waste time calling; I needed to get to Áine—and fast. My legs itched and trembled as adrenaline mixed with my element, ready for flight.

Chloe listened for a second. "No reply. I'm going to try Cú." She tried a few numbers. There was no reply from anyone. Then her phone vibrated as a text came in.

Phones to silent. Get Megan to a secure location and wait for contact.

"Shit," she muttered. "We have got to get out of here."

"I told you. Let's go!"

Chloe's phone rang. She exhaled sharply. "It's Adam." She hit the answer button. "Adam, we were just coming to look for you." Chloe's face dropped again. "Oh, it's you. Yeah, she's here. Hang on."

I grabbed the phone. "Adam?"

"It's me, Matthew."

"Matthew? What's wrong? Where's Adam? Is Áine okay?"

"I don't know. I just got back to the house, and everyone was gone. I heard Adam's phone ringing. Is everything all right? Where are you?"

I didn't answer him. I grabbed Chloe and pulled her into the air that whistled around me. "We have to get to the DeRíses'."

She screamed as I lifted us off the ground. She wriggled out of my grip and fell with a sickening crunch, dropping awkwardly on her arm. "Shit." She chewed on her bottom lip and pulled her arm to her chest. "You . . . you can't use your element openly. If there is danger around, you'll be a sitting duck." Her face paled.

"Chloe, I'm so sor—"

"No time for that. I need to get you to safety. Let's get out of here."

"I can't leave the others. We have to go to their house."

"Forget it. It's against protocol."

The wind whirled dangerously around us. "You can't stop me."

"Ugh! Fine, but from now on, listen to what I say and stop using your element. You're leaving residuals everywhere."

I jumped as Caitlin pulled up alongside us and nervously got out of the car. "What the hell is going on?" she asked, shielding herself from the vicious winds. I'd forgotten she was picking me up.

Chloe looked at her and smiled grimly.

"We're not involving her," I said.

"She's already involved. Get in," Chloe ordered, opening the back door of Caitlin's car and pushing me inside.

"Oh my god! Something's happening, right?" Caitlin said, excitement creeping into her voice as she jumped back into the car and gripped the steering wheel. "Is it the Knox?"

Chloe's jaw dropped. "You told her!"

I leaned into Caitlin's shoulder. "You remember all that life and death stuff I told you about? Well, this is it. This could get dangerous. You don't have to come."

Caitlin swallowed hard. "Where to?" She put the car into gear and pulled out with a jerk. The Micra jumped, shuddered, and cut out.

"Agh!" Chloe gasped, cradling her arm and sucking in a breath.

"Oops, sorry, I still stall when I get nervous," Caitlin muttered, turning the key in the ignition again.

Chloe finally exhaled. "The DeRíses'. And gently does it, please."

When we got there, the house was dark. As we approached the back door, Matthew emerged.

"What's going on?" he asked. "Caitlin! What are you doing here?"

"Well, I, um, well . . . hang on, what are you doing here? I thought you had gone back to the UK?"

"My flight was canceled because of the storm. I go back tomorrow. Where is everyone?"

I looked around, taking in the stillness of the yard. "I don't know. They should be here. Wait, if you decided to stay, where have you been?"

"I was just hanging ou—"

My Mark began to sting. In the next instant, I was assaulted by the Sidhe's whispers. *Danger, danger.* They swirled around me, disorienting me for a moment. "Matthew, I think we should get inside the house."

"What's wrong?" he asked.

"Go in the house. I need you all inside now."

Chloe looked at me wide-eyed, before her demeanor changed. "Megan, Caitlin, get in the house NOW!" Seeming to forget her injury, she grabbed Caitlin by the arm and shoved me toward the house.

Twenty-six

VOICES OF OLD

Danger, danger.

"Matthew!" Chloe shrieked, her good arm beckoning him toward the back door.

A slight smile curled Matthew's lips. "All right, all right, I don't know what all the fuss is about." He followed Caitlin inside.

Danger, GET OUT! The whispers became more incessant and distinct. I shook my head, trying to get clarity.

"Chloe, the Sidhe's whispers . . . they say to get out."

"What are you talking about? The safest place for us is in here, quick," Chloe demanded.

I fought against the voices telling me to leave and

struggled toward the house. Just as I reached the door, a brown, dusty haze fluttered in front of me, like a mass of dust particles caught in the sunlight, hanging in the air. *Now, get out now!* The dust shuddered and combined, taking on form. A grainy version of the Sidhe materialized, but just as he opened his mouth, the dust vanished, revealing Matthew standing in the doorway. My blood ran cold.

"Megan, what are you still doing out here? Chloe wants you inside." He smiled and held out his hand.

I eyed it suspiciously. "Something's wrong." I stumbled on the step, and Matthew reached out and steadied me. The Sidhe had tried to warn me, had attempted to appear to me. But it had all stopped. Now all I felt was the sting of danger in my Mark.

"Megan, I'm sure everything will be okay. Come inside and sit down until we can find the others."

I nodded warily and let him lead me into the kitchen.

Caitlin's face was pale. "Megan, I'm scared."

Chloe ran down the hall, slinging a leather harness over her shoulder. In the holder was a silver sword of intricate Celtic design. She checked rooms and shut doors behind her. In the kitchen, she climbed onto the counter and peered out the window. "There isn't anyone in the immediate vicinity. I need you all in an interior room. I'll keep watch."

"No, you won't."

I turned just in time to see Matthew pick up Rían's hurley club and swing it at Chloe's head. The hard white ash made contact with a sickening thud.

The impact threw Chloe forward, but she remained upright as if suspended by an invisible thread. The next few seconds felt like an eternity as I waited for Chloe to draw her sword and swoop around. She didn't. Instead, she slumped to the side, her head smacking on the countertop. Then time sped to normal, and my hearing kicked in. I wished it hadn't. All I could hear was Caitlin's scream as Chloe fell from the counter and slammed into the cold, hard tiles. She twitched for a moment and then went still.

I dragged my eyes from Chloe to Matthew. He stood with the club resting on his shoulder, wearing a grim face.

"Shit! I've never hit a girl before," he said, his voice a little tight. "I just meant to knock her out."

Anger seared through me. I threw out my arms, calling on my element. A wind swirled from my hands and shot at him, but just as it got to Matthew, it seemed to split in two, and instead of hitting him, it knocked Caitlin off her feet and broke the window on Matthew's other side.

Matthew's mouth turned up into a wry smile. "I'm afraid that isn't going to help you."

My heart thudded, and my mouth went dry. I didn't need to see it. I could feel it. Matthew had the amulet. "You've been Knox all this time?"

Caitlin, winded and trying to catch her breath, shuffled

toward Chloe on her hands and knees. "Wha . . . ," she gasped. "How could you?"

Matthew's face softened as he crouched down beside Caitlin. He ran his hand through her hair and down the side of her stricken face. "Caitie, I'm sorry. This was never supposed to involve you. You shouldn't even be here."

Caitlin cringed away from his touch.

"You're Knox," I spat. "How did we not detect you before?"

His face crinkled in disgust as he drew in a sharp breath. "I'm not Knox!" He shuddered. "I'm Order, born and raised. I'm one of the good guys. The Knox are a filthy group of power-hungry Anú worshippers. Seriously." He looked genuinely insulted. "Can you see me worshipping Anú Knox? She's one creepy chica." He laughed a little maniacally.

"She's creepy, Matthew, really? Anú's been dead for centuries."

I blocked out Caitlin's quiet sobbing, trying to call on my element again, but through my element, I could nearly taste the shield around him.

"I told you, you're wasting your time." He reached under his T-shirt and pulled out the amulet. "Fionn should have let the Order put this in the crypt." He picked up the stone and gazed at it. "Such fuss over a stupid necklace. Oh, and FYI, Anú is alive and well and, as luck would have it, is waiting to meet you."

"That's crap! Where are the DeRíses?"

"They're with Anú, of course." Matthew lifted Caitlin by the arm and gently pulled her away from Chloe. "Come on, girls, we're going for a little walk." He motioned with his head toward the door. "Ladies first."

I moved toward the scullery, scanning around me for anything I could use as a weapon.

"Don't even think about it, Megan," Matthew said behind me. "I've got Caitlin and a hurley, and I'd prefer not to use it on her."

Caitlin let out a sob.

"Nothing personal, Caitie. Let's just get through this, and we'll all go our separate ways, okay?"

We headed through the yard and into the fields behind the DeRíses' home.

I turned and caught Matthew's eye. "Why are you doing this?"

"Because I deserve better, that's why!" He sighed. "Look, I put up with all of the Order's shit. I agreed to become Áine's intended. I played by the rules. All I wanted was the easy life, and up until now, I got that."

We continued in silence across the field, the green of the grass fading to dark gray as evening descended. Grass long enough to graze our knees swayed in the light breeze that rolled in from the sea. The binding feeling of the amulet was claustrophobic. My element fought for control inside me; it wanted to attack Matthew, but it kept bouncing inward.

The sound of Caitlin whimpering made me swing around. She was slumped on the ground. "What is going on?" she said, burying her face in her hands. "Chloe could be dying, and we just left her." She looked up at Matthew with tears streaming down her face. "How can you do this? I don't understand."

"Don't waste your time worrying about a Knight," he muttered, hauling Caitlin back up.

"Get off me!" she shrieked, aiming her elbow at his nose and striking hard.

Matthew let go and grabbed at his nose as Caitlin seized her opportunity and ran to me, gripping my arm. "Run, Megan! Run!" But before she could go any farther, he dived forward and grabbed her leg. She fell with a thud into the grass.

"Don't try that again!" Matthew roared. "I'm not going to have a stupid bitch like you ruin this for me. Now move it!" He looked at his watch. "They're waiting for us."

We started forward again and crossed the stream at the bottom of the valley, working our way up the hill on the other side. It led to a flat section of the field that we used for alignment practice.

I snuck a peek at Caitlin, who was walking obediently beside Matthew, her arm locked in his grip. The blood-stained hurley rested on his shoulder like he was out for a casual Sunday stroll. Then something moved just behind them, catching my attention. The grass twitched, and a blond head flicked up for a second. Chloe! She was alive. I couldn't let Matthew see her. I needed to keep his attention on me.

"Why turn on the Order now?"

He shrugged. "Do you have any idea what it's like to grow up in a privileged world? It was great. I had everything I wanted: education, cars, holidays, and money . . . lots of money. All I had to do in return was marry Áine, but she flat-out refused. I've become very attached to my trust fund."

"This is about MONEY?" I gasped.

"Oh, don't be so shocked. You didn't really expect me to give up my way of life just because Áine decided she wasn't going to have me, did you? Oh, I agreed to play along. I even thought we might get away with it, but that Hugh guy saw right through me. He told the Order I was unfit to be Áine's intended. I was going to lose everything—my scholarship, my trust fund, the lot! A guy from the Order offered me a deal: The Knox couldn't get near you with your precious echoed lands and amulet, but if I could get the Knox the amulet and the Marked Ones, he said the Order would honor the trust."

"Someone in the Order asked you to do this? Who?" I scanned the long grass for Chloe but didn't see her. "It's not too late, you know. Get rid of the amulet, free my power, and I can help the DeRíses. We can work this out."

He nudged me on again. "You know as well as I do

there's no going back. Besides, Anú promised me a bonus on delivery. All I want is the money, and I'm outta here."

"Don't you even care what will happen to us? And to Caitlin?"

"Honestly? I do feel a little bad, but I'm not sorry. This is my ticket out, and I'm taking it. Look, you don't have to get hurt. Just give Anú what she wants."

"You know the Knights won't let this go."

He laughed. "The Knights will have bigger problems than me. Don't you see? The *Order* is doing this. They've orchestrated everything. That Anú bird wants her element back."

"Don't you care at all what will happen if the elemental power falls into the wrong hands?"

He shrugged. "Not really. This has been going on forever."

We had almost reached the practice field. A blond streak flickered across the bark of a tree before disappearing into the woods.

"How did you take the others?"

"Don't worry, I didn't hurt them. Adam, the idiot, was desolate and teary-eyed—sorry, Megan, but you could do *way* better—and they were all so preoccupied with consoling him. I just slipped the drugs the Order gave me into their tea. The Knox did the rest."

His mockery dripped like molasses from a spoon, making me want to suck the breath from his lungs and allow the nothingness to suffocate him. The ache to hurt him became unbearable.

"They didn't put up much of a fight," he said.

"You mean they couldn't put up much of a fight."

"Well, actually, I lie. Fionn put on a good show. He's a feisty old dog."

Caitlin sobbed, looking from me to Matthew, suddenly seeming small and fragile. I dug my nails into my palms. The pain helped me focus.

We came to the break in the trees that marked the end of the echoed land. A shiver ran through me as I stepped beyond the protection; the magical boundary was almost palpable in the face of the unknown.

Twenty-seven

SACRIFICES

Fresh tire tracks in the mud led us to two SUVs parked next to a ditch. My eyes flickered over their tinted windows, trying to locate Fionn and the DeRíses.

"Keep moving," Matthew ordered, putting a hand on my back and shoving me forward.

I gasped as Randel swooped down from the trees and smacked Matthew's head. Matthew grabbed him by the wing and tossed him to the side, where he landed awkwardly. "You know what, Randel? You're the most annoying of the whole lot of them!" He lashed at him with his foot, but Randel hopped out of the way.

As we passed the cars, I noticed some people huddled farther down the ditch line. My heart beat triple-time when I recognized Adam lying on the grass. Rían and Áine were beside him, a man resting a boot on Rían's head.

"Ticktock." I recognized the voice instantly. "Time is of the essence." I spun around, looking for the girl who invaded my mind. My eyes fixed on a darkened window that hummed to a close.

Suddenly we were surrounded. Five people jumped from the cars and fanned out around us. Matthew shoved Caitlin toward me. I reached out and grabbed her quivering arms. The back door of an SUV opened, and Fionn was thrown to the ground. His face was a sea of blood and swelling. His arms were bound and he struggled to stand, but his legs gave way and he fell to his knees.

A strangled sob escaped from my throat. I felt powerless as I clung to Caitlin, gazing into the dark recesses of the SUV, needing to put a face to the one who had taunted me.

"Bring it here," the voice sang.

Matthew walked to the car and pulled the amulet over his head. "I told you I'd get her."

"Shut up and give it to me," the voice demanded. A tiny white hand lashed out from the darkness and snatched the amulet from his hands before disappearing back into the shadows.

My eyes darted to Adam, Rían, and Áine. Their eyes

were open. They were alive but lay like they were paralyzed. Rían didn't even struggle when the guy who had his boot on his face leaned in farther so that his heel was in Rían's eye.

"Finally, I have it back," the voice cooed.

"And me?" Matthew said, putting his foot up on the edge of the car. "I get a bonus, right?"

"Bring her to me," the voice whispered.

Matthew stepped back and stretched out his arm to me. "There she is, in all her fourth glory." He winked.

The stupid idiot. Does he really think he's going to walk away from this?

Matthew signaled for me to join him. I ignored him and held tight to Caitlin. "Megan! Don't leave Anú waiting." He smirked.

Anú! It's not possible!

"Come, child," she instructed.

I glanced over at Fionn. I didn't know what to do.

"Anú spoke to you, girl!" a man behind me shouted before hitting me sharply between the shoulder blades.

I let Caitlin go and shuffled to the car.

"Turn around," Anú commanded as I approached the door. I slowly faced away from her.

From the corner of my eye, I saw a frail white hand reach out and grab my hair, pulling it up and revealing my neck. I shuddered as the cold skin of her finger followed the outline of my Mark. I swung around and tried to knock her hand away, but one of the guards caught my arm in a tight grip. He held my wrist and pulled me upward, nearly lifting me off the ground.

"Let go of me," I hissed through gritted teeth. I called on my element. I might not be able to use my power on the bearer of the amulet, but I was sure as hell going to use it on the others. I wrapped the air tight around the man's throat. He released my arm as I squeezed the air tighter, watching as he pulled and clawed at his neck and gasped for breath. He stumbled back, wide-eyed, turning purple. I swirled the air around us, knocking the other guards off their feet.

Eerie, childlike laughter came from the car. "Enough!"

I didn't let go of my element's grip, and the wind continued to rage around us.

"She said ENOUGH!" A guard grabbed Caitlin and held a glinting blade under her chin.

"Leave her alone!" I shouted, halting the air and dropping the grip on the guard's throat. He sucked in a huge, rasping breath and coughed.

"You stupid bitch!" he growled, lurching for me.

"Nobody touches her!" Anú snapped. The guard's face contorted with rage, and his eyes bulged, but he backed down.

I peered into the car. Anú looked like a frail child, but her face was wizened and lined like a corpse. Bits of dead flesh clung to her bones, and she was partially bald, with tufts of white and gray hair on one side of her head. Her eyes held no color. They were coal dark and lifeless. Soulless.

Matthew stepped in between us, all smiles and fake charm. "Anú, you said you wouldn't harm them, right?"

Anú didn't acknowledge that he'd spoken. Her black gaze remained fixed on me.

Matthew cleared his throat. "Anú, you have your amulet and the Marked Ones. So if it's alright with you, I want to get out of this shithole and back to civilization."

"Yes, you've proved useful." Anú pulled her hand back inside the car. A second later, the flash of a blade blinded me before it sank into Matthew's throat, slicing deep and long. I heard the blood whooshing in my head, matching the blood that gushed from the wound. He dropped to his knees, still smiling stupidly, and fell face-first into the wet dirt.

"His disrespect for the Marked was his greatest downfall. Get everyone in position," Anú ordered. "If anyone harms the fourth, they will suffer my wrath."

Two guards grabbed me on either side and held me tight. Anú leaned from the car and pointed a second silver knife at Caitlin while staring at me. "You use your element against them and I'll use this on your friend."

The guard with the purple face and bulging eyes leaned into the car and gently picked up Anú, covered her head with her hood, and carried her toward me. The amulet hung around her tiny neck, looking heavy and awkward. She slithered her hand out from the white wrap she wore and moved toward my Mark again. I cringed away from her touch and her merciless, dead eyes.

"How can you be alive?" I gasped.

Her hand paused on its way to me. I focused on it rather than look into her eyes. The milky white, paper-thin skin began to develop a haze around it, like a mist hanging on a damp field in the early morning.

She swiped her hand away and tucked it back under her white wrap. "Do I look alive to you? *You* have my life."

"I don't know what you mean."

From the confines of her guard's arms, she leaned in, put her face close to mine, and parted her lips in a feline gesture like she was going to hiss. "I am the original fourth of royal blood. It was my destiny to be the Cluaín, but the Order denied me my birthright."

Frustration boiled over in me. "Well, you're welcome to it! I never *wanted* to be a Cluaín in the first place."

Her hand shot back out and grabbed me by the neck. For someone so small and frail, her grip dug into my flesh. I tried desperately to peel her bony fingers away but couldn't. I struggled for air.

Fionn lurched for us. "Stop it!" But a swift kick in the lower back silenced him as he fell forward. Randel swooped down and clawed at the guard's face.

"Will somebody shoot that friggin bird!" the guard growled, swiping at Randel.

"No! No gunfire. Not when I'm so close. We cannot be disturbed." Anú's arm started to smoke again, the haze drifting toward my nose, where the vapor stung like acid. Black blotches blurred my vision, and my blood pounded in my ears. I fought to stay conscious. Then suddenly Anú cried out and let go, whipping her hand under the white cloth. "Do you see what they've done to me, what I'm reduced to?" she screeched, and glanced down at herself. "This body, once a vessel for great power, is being eroded to dust by the very elements it was born to hold." I cowered away from her, covering my nose, trying to make the stinging stop. Anú laughed bitterly.

"My appearance disgusts you, doesn't it, Megan? But I wear the decay like a badge of persistence. I've done what I've had to do. Being the Cluaín enabled me to take the elements of the Marked. When the Order stole my Mark, they took away my ability to hold the elements, but they couldn't take my birthright from me. I discovered I still had the power to take and absorb the elemental power. I could only hold the power for a fleeting moment, but it was enough to rejuvenate me and to prolong my existence until once again, I got the chance to do what the Order denied me. Take a good long look, Megan. You may as well get used to it, because what you see before you is your future. It's what we Cluaín do."

"I will NEVER be like you." I heaved in a breath and coughed, my lungs burning from her toxicity.

Anú turned her dead glare to Fionn. "Her ignorance is fitting for the Order. Did you not let her in on their little secret?" Anú cackled. "The Order doesn't like that part of our history, so they left it out of the translations of the Scribes. The truth is not something they like the Marked to know."

"What truth?" I asked, terrified.

"The female fourth of royal blood—the Cluaín—holds the key to the ultimate prize, the power of all five elements. You and I have the ability to combine and take the four elements and open the door to the fifth, the most powerful element of all. To enter this world, the fifth—spirit—must be borne by the fourth's royal blood. The blood of the fourth still runs deep in my veins. I will be young and beautiful again and will have the fifth element. I've earned it, living off the dregs of the Marked, taking what I could of their elements with the help of the amber shard. It kept me alive long enough in this damned life to find the next Cluaín."

"So if you can just take them, then what do you need me for?"

"Don't you see? I can only hold the powers long enough to regenerate. I'd never be able to take all four individually—I'd start to lose them before I'd taken the last. That's why I needed another Cluaín, to take all four elements in one go, and take what is rightfully mine. The Order thought they were being so clever when they killed Emma and Stephen DeRís; they thought they'd stopped the cycle of the fourth again. But they were wrong . . . as usual."

I shook my head. "No! The Knox killed them."

"Why would I kill Emma's unborn child? It was the one thing I was after. She was destined to be the next Cluaín; at least she would have been when Emma transferred her element to her, like my mother was supposed to do to me. But the Order would never have allowed it, just as they didn't for me. As soon as they discovered the child she was carrying was a girl, they sacrificed her. And in doing so, the Order lost the fourth to the Sidhe, those stupid fools. The Sidhe bided his time, waiting for the last moment to keep you hidden from all of us. That time has taken its toll on me, but it's been worth the wait. Now I have the Marked four, and the amulet is mine. I'm taking back my rightful place."

"You're lying," I said. "How could you possibly know all that?"

Anú sneered. "I know it because I lived it, you stupid girl. And you should know it too. Do you really think the Order would lose such information? The naivety of generations of Marked never ceases to amaze me. Do you really believe they lost the ability to translate texts? I've sat by for centuries, watching as the Order ruined a once-great institution with ignorance and lies, all in a bid to prolong their own existence."

Fionn lifted his head from the dirt. "Don't listen to her, Megan."

Anú glared at him. "Poor Fionn, blinded by love. You put your faith in the wrong people. I empathize with you. They betrayed me too." She nudged her guard, and he stalked closer to me. Her deathly black stare pierced me, boring right into my soul. "And you, Megan. Don't be so harsh in your judgment of me. We are one and the same."

I glared back and remained silent.

"You've tasted water, haven't you? I have too. I knew it as soon as the element was within you. It enabled our connection. Did you know each Marked leaves their own signature on the element they possess? A signature linking the generations of Marked, like a family, all waiting for the circle to come full."

"What happens when the circle comes full?"

"The Marked line comes to its end, and elements return to Danu. It's what she always intended. But the Order decided to keep the elements earthbound to prove to her that humans could handle her gift. Generation after generation, they failed. And instead of admitting their failings, and enjoying the power of the institution they reigned over, they hid the knowledge of the Cluaín with lies and rewritten Scribes, and disposed of every female fourth of royal blood or those who had the potential to become her." She swiped at my blouse, ripping it open and revealing the swirling scar left behind by Adam's element. "But they didn't get you, and your power has grown fast." She pushed my head to the side, fingering my Mark. "The fifth circle has already begun. You started the call as soon as you took your first element. Spirit is already on its way." Her eyes looked hungry. She nudged her guard again. "Quick, get everyone in position. Let's not wait a moment longer." She pointed at Fionn. "Bring the girl and the guardian with you."

I was shoved down the field to where Adam, Áine, and Rían lay motionless. Áine's eyes met mine, and her voice spoke to me in my head. *Buy time. Cú and Sebastian are coming with help. Do what you have to do to stay alive.*

I nodded in her direction and kept moving.

The guards dragged Adam, Rían, and Áine by the feet and put them into the same positions we'd practiced for the alignment.

Rían's eyes cleared a little, and he pushed himself up onto his elbows. "Get off m . . ." He collapsed back to the ground and rolled over.

"Good, they're nearly lucid," Anú said. "We must act now."

"What did you give them?" I asked.

"Just a little something our friends in the Order gave us," the bulging-eyed guard said with a leer. "Rohypnol. Apparently it's the one drug with the power to disable your elements. I'd love to give it a go on you."

"Quiet, you fool! We need her in control for the transfer," Anú said, raising a hand to his face and scratching it like a wild animal.

I scanned the trees for Chloe but didn't see her. I had to stall Anú. "How many Cluaín are there?"

She pointed a bony finger at me. "Just one. There is only one Cluaín born every fourth generation. But nobody was ever counting on me being around for longer than my own."

Two guards lined up behind Anú. Caitlin and Fionn were forced to their knees in front of the guards, with a knife at each of their throats. Caitlin's head hung low, and she whimpered. Fionn stared at Anú, his battered face defiant.

Anú pulled her hood down, revealing tufts of white-gray hair that blurred into her skin. "All you have to do is let the elements flow through you, like you've been practicing for the alignment. I'll do the rest."

"Wait! Don't you need the other Marked?" I asked. *Where are you, Chloe?*

She shook her head. "They're merely vessels. We are the Cluaín; we're the ones that matter."

"But if there can only be one, and I have the Mark, how can you be a Cluaín?"

Her face writhed with rage. "I may not bear a Mark anymore, but I'm still a Cluaín! I shall bear the fifth. It was my destiny."

"But you're not Marked anymore, so you're not *really* a Cluaín, are you? You need me."

She screeched, "I am the rightful owner of that power. You should never have received such a gift. You're not worthy!"

There was no sign of Cú, Sebastian, or Chloe. I didn't know how to begin stalling this centuries-old psycho, but I seemed to have hit a nerve in her.

I raised my chin in defiance. "I don't know about that. The Sidhe selected me. From what I hear, you had to kill your own mother to claim your Mark. That doesn't sound like rightful ownership to me."

"Ownership is ownership. Who cares if it's rightful or not? My mother was weak. She chose the Order over her own daughter. She believed in the lies. I was betrayed!" Anú spat through clenched teeth. "I don't need my Mark to get what I want. All I need is the combined power of the four elements for a few moments. I may not be able to do that by myself, but you can. When you take all four elements, you'll call upon the fifth. By the time it gets here, I'll have stripped you of your Mark and the elements you hold. All the elemental imprints in me will confuse

287

the powers. For a few moments, they will recognize me as the true Cluaín, and that will allow me to hold them just long enough to use their power to rejuvenate me and for the fifth to recognize me as the royal blood that will bear it. Now start," Anú demanded.

I glared at her. "No!"

"I command you to start!" She summoned the first guard to her. He pushed Fionn in her direction, with the blade already pressed into his throat. Blood pearled on his skin. Anú took the knife from the guard and ran her tiny fingers along the blade. "You will do this." Staring at me, she drove the knife into Fionn's side. He groaned and slowly fell to the ground.

"NO! Stop. I'll do it," I cried out, not taking my eyes off Fionn.

"Good. Because next time it will be his throat."

"I need to be touching them to do it. The elements only pass to and from me when there's physical contact."

Anú sighed. "Fine. Do what you must."

I dropped to my knees in front of Rían. "I'm so sorry. I don't know what else to do," I whispered, and took Rían's hand in mine. His eyes flared to a glowing orange as flames ignited around him. I put my other hand out and touched Áine's cheek. A tear trickled down my face as Áine's body was encased in ribbons of green and brown, and root networks and opening leaves flickered over her until she became one with the ground. Their energy burned close to me, and my own element jolted in my chest, trying to escape, wanting to join earth and fire. But to my left, burning brighter than the others, was water. I could feel Adam's element like an old friend, working its way toward me, familiar and warm.

I gazed at Adam's body, now encased in a coffin of water. His eyes burned dark and vivid behind the liquid, calling to me. I clenched my eyes shut and tried to block out the calling, until I could bear it no longer. The air whipped around me, and my eyes burst open, knowing they burned white and intense. Earth and fire gathered above my head, swirling together in a magical dance. I felt my chest open as the energy built, my element drawing the others in. Áine was first to go. She writhed and squirmed under her prison of branches and leaves until she came to a stop. The cage of growth fell away and revealed her limp and unmoving body.

"Yes, yes!" Anú's voice echoed above the noise of the storm that lashed out around us.

Rían's flames wavered, his body fighting the loss of his element. The flames lifted him from the ground, burning and raging around him until I could barely make out his form. I was crying inside, but my element reveled in the moment. It sucked the flames deep into my chest, where they roared so loud I couldn't hear my own screams.

I gasped. The water element stood beside me,

a luminescent liquid version of Adam himself. It reached out, trying to grasp my hand. I resisted, and shook my head with tears pouring down my face.

"I can't do this again, I can't, I won't. Don't do this!" I screamed at Anú.

"You can and you will," she replied.

The elements melted through me. The delicious warmth of fire mingled with the richness of earth and the coolness of water. I felt . . . complete. Immensely powerful. And I hated myself for it. But the feelings swelled up inside of me, seeping into my brain, pushing past any hatred, doubt, and sadness.

"It's amazing, isn't it?" Anú's haunting voice whispered in my ear. I turned to face her. In one swift movement, she pulled the amulet from her neck, threw it around mine, and grabbed my hand. "Now it's my turn."

Pain shuddered through me. My chest dragged forward with such strength that I thought my body had split in two. It was like the searing pain I had felt when Adam's element had returned to him, only worse . . . much worse. Death would be a relief, but instead the agony continued and the elements proceeded to drain from me.

A light shone out of my chest and swirled around me, rippling over my skin. I could sense the elements resisting, pausing where her hand met mine, as if they weren't quite sure. Then they started to seep into her. She jerked at first, convulsing as the power slowly melted into her. I watched in amazement as her body lengthened and filled out, her skin warming and turning a peachy tone.

Then from the corner of my eye, I spotted Chloe. She crept up behind Anú's guard, sword at the ready, and felled him with one stroke. The other guards were so enraptured by the display, they didn't see her approaching. She dived at us and snapped the amulet from my neck. Like springs recoiling, the elements spiraled through the air and smashed simultaneously into Anú and me, throwing us to the ground and forcing our hands apart. Everything was silent for a few moments.

Then, just in front of us, a crack appeared in the atmosphere. A powerful light ripped through it, slicing through the air like it was cutting through fabric.

"What has she done?" Anú screeched, pulling wildly at her still-white hair. "The transfer wasn't complete!"

Twenty-eight

THE FIFTH

With a flick of Anú's hand, she formed a magical wall of water that curved up around us, imprisoning her, Chloe, and me with the light that sliced through the air, which was getting bigger every second. Just before the dome closed completely, Randel dived through the gap and swooped on Anú. He went straight for her face, gouging at her eyes. Anú shrieked and slapped at the fluttering black wings, flinging him back, but he came at her again. Water formed on Anú's hand. She threw the liquid at Randel. Midair, it formed into an icy dagger, hitting Randel clear in the chest. He dropped to the ground with a thump, unmoving. His bright black eyes dulled, staring vacantly.

My heart felt like it was cracking as I stared at Randel. I could see Fionn hammering on the wall of water. The faint thud of his fists sounded far away as he slid down, landing in a heap at the base.

Chloe moved toward us, holding the amulet to her chest with her injured arm. The glinting steel of her blade reflected the brilliant light that was now ripping its way into the world. "You have no power over me."

With the back of her hand, Anú wiped the blood that oozed from her eye and smeared it on her white dress.

"Put the amulet back on, Megan," Anú snarled.

"So you can kill me?" Chloe said, moving closer.

Anú's eyes flicked to the glowing fissure. "We need to finish the transfer. The elements are still split; we must correct that before it comes."

"Before what comes?"

"The fifth. Spirit. Put it on, Megan. NOW."

The four elements fizzed under my skin, confused and incomplete. I tried to connect to the strange sensation. It was like they'd been halved somehow. If Anú could use them, I should be able to as well, but I still struggled. It was like my link to them had been severed. The air crackled around us, and I felt drawn to Anú. The elements wanted to be whole again.

Anú screamed and lurched to one side. "I can't hold on to the power for much longer. You MUST complete the transfer."

"How do we stop the fifth?" I asked.

Anú growled. "Do you think we can seal a crack between worlds? Once the fifth is called upon, it comes. As soon as you combined the elements, you invited it here. And when it arrives, it will be looking for the Cluaín to bear it. I was Marked, so I can channel the powers just long enough to receive the fifth, but I can't hold on to elements for too long." Her eyes searched me. "I swear to you, I won't harm the other Marked. They'll get their elements back. All I want is the fifth." She licked her lips and reached out her hand to Chloe, eyeing the amulet hungrily. "Chloe, you'll be saving Megan from the sacrifice she'd have to make; you know the fifth has to die before it can live. I'm willing to do that for the power of the fifth element, to be Marked once again."

"So what, you're going to sacrifice Megan now?" Chloe asked. "Because I know there's no way you'll let her live."

"Either way, Megan will perish. You know what will happen when she gives in to the call of the fifth. Nothing will change that outcome. Chloe, I can offer you so much more than the Knights can. Join me. Be part of something bigger."

Chloe lowered her sword in front of her, and my heart stopped. *She can't possibly be considering this, can she?*

Then she stepped closer to Anú. "Never," she whispered, and in one swift movement, she slid her sword through Anú's chest.

"Stupid girl," Anú howled, dropping to the ground and knocking the amulet from Chloe's hands. "You leave me no choice!" Anú twisted her arm in the air, and a sphere of water pulled away from the liquid wall. It moved sluggishly, like hot wax in oil, and enveloped Chloe's body. Chloe fought to remove it—pushing it, pulling it, and dropping to the ground, trying to shake it off—while her horrified face battled for air. Her hand reached for the amulet, but the water bubble held strong, not allowing her to grip it. I tried to call on the water element to stop it, but it didn't respond.

Anú gripped the sword and pulled it from her body with a grunt. Then she turned to me. "You have it in you to save her. Put the amulet back on. Finish the transfer. Your life for hers."

I stared in horror at Chloe's now-purple face as she continued to struggle, and I went to retrieve the amulet, but Chloe stumbled in front of me and shook her head.

"Put it back on!" Anú shrieked.

Chloe stopped fighting, put her foot over the amulet, and looked me straight in the eye. She smiled sadly, then took a big breath of water. Her body jolted backward, and then she did it again and fell to the ground. I couldn't look anymore. Anú lurched to the side like there was a magnetic field pulling us together. As soon as her skin made contact with mine, I felt her lose her grip on the elements. Suddenly fire was coursing through me. The heat grew at my core, intensifying until I could no longer contain it. Searing heat and flames filled the air, forming a giant halo that burned through the wall of water. The halo moved rapidly upward, evaporating the water before it could fall. Outside the ring of flames, the fight was raging. Sebastian and Cú had finally arrived with reinforcements and were busy taking down the last of the Knox. I turned my glare to the now-powerless Anú, who looked small and fragile as she lay curled up on the ground, clutching her bleeding stomach.

"You lose," I said.

Anú pointed behind me. "Not yet, I haven't."

The fissure had grown. A bright yellow light pushed it wider. Among the light, a spinning ball of lumini-ous gray particles moved upward. It hovered for a few moments, then pulled apart, forming two spheres—one light, the other dark. The fissure behind them sealed with an ear-splitting crash.

The white sphere rushed at me. I threw out all the elements at once, trying to shield myself, but it pow-ered through them all. I braced myself for impact, but it never came. The sphere dissolved on contact. I gasped as a tingling sensation began at my center and rippled out. Everything got very bright, and for a moment, I was blinded. I squeezed my eyes closed against the glare. As the sensation finally ebbed, I dared to look again. Anú was edging forward as the dark sphere moved around me, curling along my limbs as if it were seeking an entry.

"The fifth separated! It must have sensed the two Cluaíns and separated!" Anú laughed hysterically. She put out her hands and beckoned to the dark sphere. "No! Come to me. I'm the one you seek. I will make you whole again. Together we will make the circle come full."

The swirling ball of mist stopped moving over my body. It suddenly raced at Anú, forcing itself into her mouth, stretching it wider and wider until Anú's face was completely distorted. Anú screamed and staggered toward the wall of fire that still burned brightly. Her eyes opened wide with terror as she ran toward it, melting into the flames. Her cries blended into the roar of the inferno; the two were indistinguishable. Anú's charred bones fell into a heap with a hollow knocking sound as the mist started to swirl and form back into a sphere. My heart beat wildly as the sphere moved back toward me. I didn't dare breathe. Then it glided away across the grass, stopping abruptly at Chloe's body. It started moving erratically, nudging her like a curious animal. Suddenly the mist spread out over her body, smothering it for a moment, and then it sank into her skin. As it did, Chloe twitched. Her head darted from side to side until her chin pointed to the sky and her body stretched out with a jolt. Her face scrunched up and her eyes shot open as a dark ripple glided across her features.

Then I watched in awed horror as Chloe sat forward, coughing up water and then gasping for breath.

Cú raced past me and scooped Chloe up in his arms. "I thought you were dead. I thought you were dead," he repeated over and over with a broken voice. "I'm so sorry."

Caitlin ran to my side and tugged my arm. "You better come quick."

She guided me to Fionn, and I dropped to my knees beside him. "Fionn!" The wind whipped up around me, and the clouds descended, low, dark, and swirling. Thunder crashed and lightning snapped at the sky, striking a hay barn the next field over, engulfing it in flames.

I put my hands on his face. Áine had been able to heal animals before. Maybe it could work for people too. I took another deep breath and focused all my energy on him, struggling to get a grip on the elements whirling inside me. The trees loomed over me, their limbs reaching for my arms and body, wrapping themselves around me in an embrace.

I felt Áine's compassion and emotion flow through the branches as they hugged me. The heat of Rían's fire radiated off my skin, followed by rain, gentle and soft. I could not mistake Adam's caress in the water that trickled over my body. I breathed deeply and exhaled long and hard until there wasn't an ounce of air left in my system. I lost myself to the comfort that Áine, Adam, and Rían gave me and leaned down to Fionn. "Please don't leave us," I whispered. I felt so small as I cradled his head in my arms, willing some of the elemental comfort into what life remained in him. A shallow, gurgled breath escaped his lips. I dared to hope, waiting for the next one. But it didn't come.

I looked at the distraught faces around me. "Someone do something!" I leaned on Fionn's chest, started doing chest compressions, and watched as blood trickled from his mouth. "Help me!!"

A hand rested on my shoulder. "Megan, his injuries were too severe. He's gone."

I whipped my head around and saw Sebastian standing behind me. "You haven't even tried!"

He kneeled down beside me. "He's gone, Megan. We have to take him now. We have to clear the field of all evidence of what happened here today."

The tears gushed down my face as I looked over to where Adam, Rían, and Áine lay. "They never got a chance to say good-bye to their mother and father— please, give them the chance to say good-bye to Fionn. They deserve that. Fionn deserves that."

He nodded sadly and waved away the group of Knights that were moving in on us. "Get the Marked."

I turned back to Fionn and slowly ran a hand down his disfigured face. There were so many emotions streaming through me. I gently closed his glazed eyes and whispered my good-byes as the Knights carried Adam, Áine, and Rían to us. I got up as they approached and left the DeRíses lying unconscious beside their dead guardian.

"You'll be needing this," Cú said, holding the amulet over my head. I nodded and bent down to run the back of my hand along Adam's cheek.

"Are you sure you want to do this now?"

"Yes." I reached out and allowed my arms to gently graze over Adam, Áine, and Rían's skin. Cú dropped the chain around my neck and stepped back. Pain shot through me instantly, triple in strength, but it was a relief. I connected with it and watched as the curling symbols burned into my skin. Now I had all four. The elements flickered through the air like a firework display, creating beautiful patterns as they crisscrossed before diving for the chests of their owners. Their bodies arched forward to receive their elements. The pain began to ease.

Adam, Áine, and Rían woke up confused, and I had to turn away when their eyes focused on Fionn's body.

Caitlin dropped down beside me and wrapped me in a hug. Through the fog of pain and grief, the shock of seeing Petra holding Chloe tenderly in the distance barely registered. They were joined by Hugh as they approached us.

Petra spoke softly. "Caitlin, this is Hugh. He'll look after you."

Caitlin shot me a nervous glance. "Megan?"

I looked deep into Hugh's forlorn, tear-filled eyes

and knew immediately we could trust him. "It's okay, Caitlin. Go with Hugh, I'll be with you in a second."

As Hugh led Caitlin away from the chaos I glanced warily at Petra. "Who are you?"

"I am the same person you've always known."

"You're Order?"

She shrugged. "Sort of. I'm a member of the Ciorcal na Fírinne, the Circle of Truth. We're a side of the Order who believe it's time to let the circle come full, like Danu intended. To allow the Cluaín to return the elements to their rightful place."

"What about the alignment?"

"The time for that has long since passed. The Council has been preventing the inevitable for centuries. As soon as you've done your job, the alignments will no longer be your concern. I've been watching the DeRíses since the Order killed their parents. The Order was too hasty in their disposal of the new Cluaín. She hadn't been born yet, so there was still a chance for the Cluaín of this generation. The Sidhe had the opportunity to activate a Mark and hide the Cluaín in you until the time had come for the full circle. I gave up my old life and moved with the DeRíses, knowing that someday the Cluaín would show up."

"You knew this would happen?"

She looked around sadly. "No, not this. But we knew the age of the fifth was upon us, and we had to be here to protect you from the Council and those in the Order who are loyal to them. They'll do anything to stop the full circle, even let Anú in to do their dirty work. That one backfired on them, though."

"How so?"

"They thought she just wanted to drain your element. That she'd steal your power and leave you for dead the way she did with all the other Marked she'd taken. They were willing to sacrifice you, the DeRíses, and their precious alignment if it meant the continuation of the Marked line on Earth and the existence of the Order. But what they didn't know was that Anú was seeking the very thing the Order was trying to avoid. The release of the fifth."

I glanced over at the distraught faces of the DeRíses. Áine was crouched over Fionn's body. I felt what was left of my heart shatter into a million pieces. "What does this all mean?"

Petra sighed. "This means everything has changed. Everything."

Twenty-nine

EPILOGUE

Petra was right. Everything did change.

Within two days, the Order had removed all trace of the Knox and Fionn's death. The hurricane debris had been cleared, repairs were underway, and power had been restored to town.

Cú decided to stay in Kinsale for as long as Adam, Rían, and Áine wanted him there, and Sebastian and Chloe stayed too. Chloe was working through what had happened to her, but we still hadn't spoken about it. There were whispers of a split in the Order and sides being taken, but I had more pressing worries. Adam had yet to come out of his room, and school was starting again the next day.

I knocked on the door and walked in before Adam answered. He sat on the side of his bed with his shoulders hunched forward, gazing out at the fields beyond.

His element hung heavy in the air like a cloud of humidity. I perched on the windowsill that was just outside the reach of his power.

"Afraid to even sit with me now?" Adam asked, his eyes still fixed on the horizon behind me.

"Of course not." I got up and moved toward him, forcing his eyes to focus on me. His face was like stone, chiseled in anger. "Adam, please don't be mad at me."

"At you!" A bitter laugh escaped his throat. "I'm not mad at *you*." The air grew heavier. The humidity cloud moved closer to me, and beads of moisture began to form on my skin. "I hate them—the Order—for what they did to you, to my parents, to F . . . Fionn." His voice broke as his chin dropped to his chest. "I miss him," he whispered. He hugged himself tight, breathing deeply and slowly as the cloud of element magic around him shrank, pulling closer and closer to him until it was just the slightest haze that dusted his skin.

I kneeled on the ground in front of him and put my arms next to him, feeling the tickle of warmth from his skin. "Me too."

I moved my face close to his. Just the gentle caress of his breath on my face made me feel better. But it was too pleasant, too familiar. The urge to throw myself into his arms was overpowering. I pulled away and made my way to the door, feeling the tears trickle down my cheeks. "I'm so sorry, Adam, I'm so—"

"I know," he snapped as his element sprang back out around him. I could taste the bitter taint of hurt, sadness, and revenge that infused the air as it followed me out of the room.

The door slammed behind me as I left. I leaned against it, swallowing back the sobs I felt rising in my throat. Tears welled in my eyes, and I quickly wiped them away, not allowing myself the indulgence of crying. I took a deep breath and felt a resolve come over me. My future was uncertain, but the one thing I was sure of was that the pain and hurt had to stop. And if I could do that by being the Cluaín, I was going to do everything in my power to make the circle come full. This time, the Order would lose.

The Marked line would end with me.

ACKNOWLEDGMENTS

Huge thanks to my editor, Erica Sussman, for believing in me and inviting me into a world beyond my wildest dreams. Thanks also to Tyler and the team at HarperTeen. I've adored every minute of working with you.

To my agent, Tina Wexler, thank you for your wisdom and gentle guidance. Your encouragement means so much to me.

Thank you to all the bloggers, reviewers, fans, and my online friends who have cheered me on from the start, you guys shine so brightly and carry me through the tough times. Honestly, you've no idea how much your enthusiasm means to me.

To my critique partners and readers, especially Morgan Shamy, Wendy Higgins, Jennifer L. Armentrout, and my sis, Jen Galvin, thank you for putting up with my horrible first drafts. You guys rock my world.

Thanks to my street team, Mom, Dad, Jenny, Denis, Betty, Emma, Kate, and various extended family and neighbors who have been on hand to help out while I've been away from home. I couldn't have done it without you all. And of course to my ever-amazing husband, Michael, and my children, Chloe, Megan, Fionn, and Rían, thank you for your endless support and love. I adore you all.

Lastly, thanks to my neighbors, the Morins, who kindly donated the use of their garage and generator after Hurricane Irene robbed me of power for a whole week just as my deadline approached. Never again will I laugh at people who store just-in-case water, tinned food, weapons, and fuel in a fall out shelter. I know where I'm running to when the zombie apocalypse strikes.

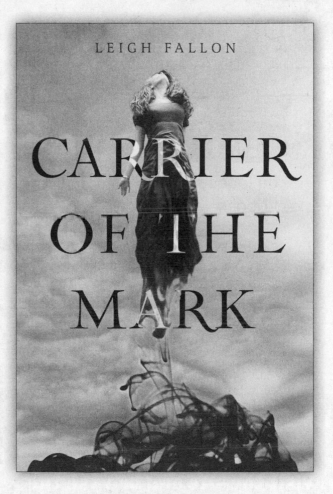